How to Paint an American

ANDREW McGREGOR

Fresh Ink Group
Guntersville

How to Paint an American

Fresh Ink Group
An Imprint of:
The Fresh Ink Group, LLC
1021 Blount Avenue #931
Guntersville, AL 35976
Email: info@FreshInkGroup.com
FreshInkGroup.com

Edition 1.0 2023

Cover art by Keith Wong
Author photo by Jonathan Moore
Covers by Stephen Geez / FIG
Book design by Amit Dey / FIG
Associate publisher Beem Weeks / FIG

Cataloging-in-Publication Recommendations:
FIC069000 Fiction / City Life
FIC130000 Fiction / Diversity & Multicultural
FIC084040 Fiction World Literature / American / 21st Century

Library of Congress Control Number: 2023901792

ISBN-13: 978-1-958922-13-2 Papercover
ISBN-13: 978-1-958922-14-9 Hardcover
ISBN-13: 978-1-958922-15-6 Ebooks

*I dedicate this book to my parents,
the mother- and fatherlands with their tectonic
powers to shape a world.*

Acknowledgements

Thank you very much to all the people in all the exquisite, cruel, and exotic places who shared adventures with me by day and heartfelt (and fought) wisdom by night. When asked how I thought of this book, I think of you and our flood of memories that have since washed away to time's transfixing ocean.

Thank you to the great and good publisher Gary "Stephen Geez" and his maestro editor Beem Weeks for the many hours over many nights to help finally forge the thing. A thousand thanks to Keith Wong for cover art most sublime. Enduring gratitude to Jonathan Moore for lending his vast photographic talents for the author's picture.

The following people make up the texture of my daily "why," and I am profoundly grateful for the gift of your gravity on my life: blessed siblings Alison and Molly, magnificent Aunt Anne, and those devoted Canadian summers; and Eric Coble, the finest high-school teacher Yale ever hurled to Colorado. Mr. Walton, Larry Vogel, and Kristin Pfefferkorn; Michael Parks (RIP) and KC Cole; Edinburgh's finest in Peter Black and Typewronger Books, and its devoted owner, Tom Hodges; Professor Kuan-ju Wu, Kim Ngo, Douglas Campbell, Chet Udell, Daniela Kon, the wonderful Jason Risk—who was unexpectedly ripped from us; Daunia Arena, Valentina, e tutta La Puglia, grazie mille.

Jed Smith, Janna Avner, Bahar İrfan, Alexa Meade, Lora Miro, Paul Debevec, Rick Meyer, Sonia Kazarova, Ross Mead, Nathan Cartwright, Bill Dorrman, Paul Weiss, David Guida, Pax Franchot, Anne Milasincic Andrews, Barrett Morse, Arsen Petrosyan, Braden McDorman, Justin Fortune, Tamara Frapasella, Antoni Hardonk, Liefia Ingalls, Ned Vizzini (RIP), Coleman Hough, Logan Gelbrich, John Odden, Richard Gibbs, Max Gail, Jr., the chaps at the Adventurers' Club of Los Angeles, Tony Lugo, Gina Levy, Laurent Malaquais, Barrett Morse, Gina Nahai, Stephanie Pellegrini, Leslie DiLullo, Robert Proctor, Chantelle Dinkel, Dierdre Martin, Elizabeth Amini, Justin Kessler (RIP), Ted Jessup, Aaron Shaw, Martin Winter, Zhanibek Amanov, Lamon Brewster, Chris Berotti, Vin Merola, Eduardo Del Signore, Richard Gibbs, Marshall Porter, Timur Gareyev, Marcel Dejure, Shelita Burke, Gerard Egan, Carolyn Sills, Kristin Burke, Jean-luc Dushime, Solange Nyamulisa, Malte Hagermeister, Wilson Owen Wilson, Reed Harris, Chad Allen, Will Richter, and Richard Ballard.

Of course, also you, dearest reader.

Thank you all for all the things!

Table of Contents

Song 1

Verse 1

A woman's dusty, red-heeled shoe spiraled down in awkward pirouettes from the near haze of the sky before hitting the ground slower than it should have. Clouds of marauding dust and cement followed behind and turned life into night. The day of 9/11 had not yet concluded and something else entirely was being born in the moment: A fetus of the rapture, wrought by a time it never wanted.

A man sat choking in a dust silhouette. He was unable to breathe because of the events unfolding around him. His time had passed. He had had his moment in the Vietnam War that left shining cat's claws across his back. Now he was in another moment, a more important one in which he was stoically choking, for it was the future—a time of indiscriminate terror and detente. It was a way life after the war—at least for *him*—except now he could taste it in suffocating gasps; the remnants of fire and coated breath coagulated in his mouth. He thanked God that he was not born in New York so he could die away from the land of his birth. The amorphous dark he could not recall was more terrifying than the sizzling dust dancing across his nostrils, singing the melancholic tomes of eternity in his ears.

Later he would stumble blindly to a bar and drink single-malt scotch on the house. A first for him. Now he had his moment. New York was bigger than eternity—that was the joy of the whole thing—but it was not bigger than this moment. The world was not bigger than this moment. So, he prayed at the altar of the bar for the drink to help him escape, for the high-class oblivion from the shaman. He prayed hard now, and for the rest of this day, until night became night again and a wayward star would pierce through the towering skyline and curiously wonder what had changed in the land of parched light below.

The scotch mixed with the ash he could not remove and startled him with its acrid awfulness. It was something tart and more expensive than he could have ever wanted. He thought about the tragedy of this tale. Prior to the cascading shadows of dust and death, New York was a place that ensured obscurity so everyone sought a safe niche they could call identity. Lives were lived and spent ultimately to be in a place, to have an identity in *this* place. In any other place he would have been a better man, but here he was nothing. He could be nothing no matter how talented he was. That was the joy of it all.

This tale was not about him, though. It was not about this moment, either. There was something to come before he was finished with his life and this city, before he could die—something important he could never remember because it was not what he had been trained to seek.

Down the bar a grown man wept, consoled by no one because everyone else was buried in each other's arms. He was the odd number because Jerome Ironside, the man with the Scotch, would not move. He would do nothing the rest of the day but drink and weep when the ice cube he had been staring at melted without his really noticing.

It had all been wrong: his life, his dreams, his reality. So, he wept and toasted to himself in praise of a life not quite wasted but not well-chosen. Then a gulp and a toast to the tragedy that was beyond face and comprehension. It would remain incomprehensible until that day when he would stand stark before a rising sun and realize that he had done something of consequence and that it all had an end, something that would endure long after he had washed the ash of America's longest night down a clockwise drain.

A man of several baptisms, by ash and by water, the rest of his life he would wait for the final one—the only baptism he could love, that day when the sun would set and would never rise because he would not be there to see it. On that day he could finally curse the duality that had spawned him: his God and His city.

Verse 2

Jiři Slävøvic exited the concourse to a bright springtime day at JFK International Airport, exhausted and euphoric. He had never been on a plane before and after experiencing it he never wanted to be on one again. He was a man of mixed European ancestry and multiple fathers. A biological result of the great war, that Teutonic tumbling of dice that created modern Europe. He sometimes wanted to describe himself only as what he knew his mother to be, but his Slavic nature prevented this. Jiři's mother was spawned by the hapless romance of two slain lovers from warring political factions. She never told Jiři which specific movements they were from, but their drive to martyrdom was something she regretted his not having.

He needed a father in his cultural recollection, if not in his life, and she failed him in this great spiritual undertaking. To rebel he traced his lineage to the language he was currently speaking (in this case Czech), yet since he could never muster the energy to speak it very well, he considered himself only one-third Czech.

The rest of him would have to be American since he had been studying English under a wan light at his dusty desk in Prague. He could have passed for a Brit but decided that if he were to do that he might as well say he was Australian. So, he would be Czech until someone could tell him better. The flight over from Prague had a two-hour layover in Germany, and he was debating whether or not to say he was German. Jiři's first father spoke German, so he did as well, but he did not know any Germans.

Behind him the stagnant air of a thousand indifferent travelers clogged his past. Like mountain tops piercing clouds, a million heads bobbed in unharmonious unison before him. With a tweak of his newly graying mustache and a tug on his duffel bag, he headed forward with no plans, money, or reservations. He believed only a few things. He believed that the world was a tender, but cruel place. He also believed that very few things were worth fighting for—and fewer still worth dying for. He also believed that he would find what those things were in America.

He chuckled as he noticed the people staring at him. He wore green coveralls atop a blue-striped sailor shirt that offended his mother because she said it made him look Russian. Satisfied, he smiled. If he could be a foreigner in New York City, then he could be a foreigner anywhere.

Sliding automatic doors opened and released a deluge of noise that stopped the English-language learning tapes spinning in his memory. The nascent winter humidity stifled and choked him with misty pollution and a coat of atmosphere. He furtively rifled through the wad of American money that his rich dead uncle had given him ten years ago and then boarded a bus headed towards the gothic-looking columns jaggedly piercing the sky.

As the bus shook, he was crammed into a pew-like seat. Jiři remembered being in church when he was a child—before his parents changed their minds and decided not to attend anymore. Everywhere he found himself seemed as large as the first day of school. This sensation looped and looped. Jiři knew then that he was only looking at the knees of God and that when he was older, he would be able to see higher things. He had once asked one of his fathers about it and received a loving smack on the back of the neck that confirmed Jiři's suspicions that he was correct.

Now he was hot and confused and unsure of where God's body began and ended as the tops of the buildings extended beyond what he could see through the steamed window of the bus. Windows of apartments flashed by, and he thought of those thousands of souls all stacked in concrete. He wondered if Americans ever ate sardines and if they did could they ever see themselves through the prism of those fish all lying together beneath the coffin lid bearing their eternal brand.

The Port Authority looked less impressive than in his uncertain imagination. Below his feet the bus stopped and the people exited. So, he did as well. Finding a nearby bench he sat, back erect, and surveyed the crowd while thumbing the inchoate gray hairs on his mustache. He smiled. It tickled his upper lip, sensing the exquisiteness of being an individual in a place where nobody had his Czech mustache. Since he was one-of-a-kind, he knew that the American women would crave him.

Outside, the sterile fluorescent lighting of city life changed as time wandered into an early dusk. A man sitting across from Jiři looked impressed with his stature, outfit, and mustache. Because of this, Jiři imagined the man making a silent deal with him. If he could smoke three generous piles of tobacco from his pipe before Jiři left, he would know his heart, befriend him, and send him on a journey.

After he inhaled the second pile of tobacco, he formulated his plan. This rare occasion gave him joy for it was an occasion for him to acquire another anecdote for his community-college class where no one would question the studies he cited from the 1930s, the ones he made up about Eastern European immigrants who were separated from their culture by the always nefarious United States government and then forced to do things for which they could not know the consequences. In another life he would have been a better man because he would have worked for a better life. However, he had never really cared for hardship because he did not care about anything.

He gazed at Jiři, this thing approaching his thirties in overalls and a sailor shirt. He was about to receive his mission . . . from God or something else. The causes of things really did not matter since it was what he was waiting for anyway.

He cast the ash from his pipe to the ground and walked across the station. Jiři grew larger in his eyes and mind with each step until he stood before him and stared like a child seeing a new kind of animal for the first time. He became uncomfortable so he sat next to him and again felt himself to be his equal.

He looked up to Jiři and said, "Does it make you ashamed to be white?"

Jiři could not hear him. He was focused on something beyond the wall. In Prague, he had heard an American expatriate say that all he had to do to get a woman was sit at a café and place his passport in front of him. Sometimes, he wanted to attach it at the end of a fishing pole and wave it about until someone bit it. Jiři never saw that American again nor did he speak to him. Yet, the idea of catching a woman by tying papers to a pole intrigued him.

Being a stranger in a city of strangers, Jiři mulled the possibilities and thought that an unbaited net would probably be a better form of introduction to the women here. Abruptly, he was interrupted by a verbal tug on his right ear. "Does it make you ashamed to be white?"

Jiři gazed into his eyes, seeking comprehension, and the man flinched. He knew the words, but their sequence was baffling. A piece of white paper fluttered at his feet, an advertisement for a punk band and a Spanish-speaking mortgage agency. There was no printing on the back, so Jiři pointed to that and said the word white.

"Yes, aren't you ashamed of it?"

"This paper is not mine. You want?" With the eyes of an invincible deer, Jiři handed him the whiteness in his hand. The man took it and fastidiously folded it into a sloppy polygon.

"Thanks, but I got my own at home."

"Good." Jiři continued to look into the stranger's eyes while they darted and prodded him from his ankles to his neck. It all made Jiři wonder why the man would not look at his virulent mustache.

"Where you from?"

"I am from Prague."

"Really, I can never tell with you people and your accents, wish you were more like the British. Then again, those Australians sound the same to me."

"I do not have accent." For Jiři this was true, as the language tapes he continually played in his skull matched the English that flowed from his mouth. A poor but happy friend of his had once been shipped to New York to paint a magnificent Christ on the wall of a rich woman's home. It was his best work and he hated letting her have it. His friend said that the accents in New York would change with each street. He said that America is a labyrinth and in the center there must be the true form of English and that if you can touch it you will feel the purity of an American spirit.

The man spoke again and shattered Jiři's memory of his poor and happy friend. "How would you know?"

"I hear the tapes in my head, and I am the same."

The man chuckled without smiling. "What are you doing here?"

"I am sitting and waiting and watching." Jiři's eyes had returned to what existed beyond the wall.

"Nah, man. I mean, what are you doing in New York in a bus station right here and right now?"

Jiří did not believe in fate. He also did not believe himself to be intelligent or powerful enough to create a destiny of his own. There were too many other people to let that happen. He believed in something else that was not in between but beyond.

"I am here to learn the American way of things and to have my one great adventure."

"You're here for an adventure."

"I believe."

"All right. Where are you staying?" The stranger paused then continued. "What hotel do you plan on sleeping in tonight?"

"I do not know—whatever one finds me."

"You can stay at my place, man. Then I'll give you a journey."

"I want an adventure, not a journey."

"There's a difference?"

"Yes!" Jiří shouted.

"Okay, okay, I'll give you your adventure. What's your name?"

"Jiří Slävøvic."

"What?"

"Jiří Slävøvic."

"Um, yeah, no one here will ever be able to say that name unless they cut their tongues in two. You are in America now. Your name is Uri, cool with that? Let's ride."

"Uri is Russian name."

"What?"

"I am not Russian. I am from Prague now—but before, I was something else. Still, I am not Russian."

"Well, in the next life, Prague can win some wars and force humanity to pronounce that word. To the victor go the spoils, as the Whites will say. You are Uri, a Russian, born again in America."

The two nodded at each other with codependent contempt. The man introduced himself as Jerome Ironside and told Uri that he had grown up in the northern Bronx but now lived in Brooklyn. Uri nodded his head and asked if he was from New York and Jerome said that he was.

Walking away from the bus station Jerome thought about carrying Uri's duffel bag and then changed his mind. The fabric of the handle was stretched to the precipice of breaking and Uri's long, smooth strides showed no effort as he carried the enormous weight.

"C'mon, man. Let's hit the subway." Jerome dashed underground while Uri stood and looked straight up at the surrounding buildings. It reminded him of an intergalactic gala streaming through space with no real landmarks—only glowing squares attached to cement, looking at other glowing squares across the street. The entire thing made Uri feel dizzy.

"Yo! Let's hit the subway." Uri had stayed at the top of the entrance looking at the interstellar city that was so bright it blocked out the stars. Jerome yelled at him rather than walking back up the stairs. Perhaps it had to do with his upbringing.

"You do not have car?"

"No."

"This is America. Everyone has car."

"True, but *this* ain't America. *This* is Neeew York." His head jerked up like a desert lizard basking in the noonday sun. A passerby in a giant puffy ski coat offered Jerome his fist and he pumped it back with his own in a seamless exchange amidst the symphonic movement of chaotic millions.

Uri's duffel bag groaned, and he descended while trying to think of the English meaning of the words listed on the street signs before going under and leaving all that was extraordinary and new behind. He vowed not to forget it before what was next—the future. He hoped it would not unravel him before he obtained what he came here seeking.

Verse 3

The shimmying of the subway car made Uri believe that it would collapse if he stood too quickly. Everywhere he looked he saw advertisements and they caused him to divert his eyes to the floor. A gentle tug on his duffel bag indicated that he should leave the subway car with Jerome.

Above the endless tunnels through which the city breathed its humanity, Uri looked up and was surprised to see flecks of stars above. All the grand cement monoliths were gone. They had been replaced by stubby buildings that were all similar in their indistinct facades. The people were different. They cowered. The energetic motion from the other part of the city had left them. Uri felt he had arrived in a new country and asked Jerome if it was true. Jerome replied that they were in New York and that the little kid from the hills would have to get used to city life. Uri thought about telling him that he was from Prague but was distracted by Jerome pulling on his arm—like a prison guard—yanking him down the street.

The silence of the place startled him. "C'mon." Jerome walked forward, quickly and in silence. Uri had to exert himself to keep up. He was certain that if he fell behind Jerome would never turn around to find him. He thought back to the story of Orpheus and Eurydice he had been told in a violent bar as a child.

Jerome's home cast a shadow away from the streetlights. Uri could see more stars, but he could not see where he was going.

A door cracked open. A light came on and a shadow that looked like a demon puppet emerged.

"Like the digs, man?" Jerome said.

The room was both spartan and better than anything Uri had known. Uri's entire mustache smiled.

Jerome smiled back and said, "I'm glad there's a few happy honkeys floating around after all."

Jerome excused himself, saying that he had work to do, and that the bathroom was down the hall, and that he was sure Uri would find it if he exerted enough effort. The sound of the door quickly shutting barely reverberated in Uri's ears as he started to remove all his clothes. His mustache danced, and he understood what butterflies must feel when the winter months end and at last they can exist, born again.

For the first time in his life he felt a sense of privacy. He stripped until he was naked, except for his socks, and kicked his clothes into a pile in the corner. He would always keep his feet covered, as he viewed them as two kittens that had to remain warm lest the world corrupt them and strip them of their adorableness.

Behind Uri's door separating himself from the world, the muffled, hammering report of a typewriter dashed through the whiteness of a thin sheet of off-white paper, filling the pages with a government document that was never written, as far as Jerome knew, but that seemed to him like someone should have—given the zeitgeist of those times.

Incessant reading had driven illusions of creativity out of Jerome, but he still carved joy from this hammering of the keys. It was his practice to recreate what was so obviously apparent in retrospect but flagrantly ignored by his own culture's memory. Instead of forgetting inconvenient truths, Jerome worked to create reasonable lies to show a map to the present.

His typing became more erratic until his concentration waned and massive, peculiar typos started appearing, the kind he imagined that Uri would write. A razor slash of sound cut the air as he removed one page and floated it to the floor and frantically loaded the next. He vowed that this page would have no mistakes and no typos. This page would be an act of Zen and passion:

> Report on the Communist Incursions and Infiltration of
> New York City through Spurious Defections.

Yes, he thought, *that has a nice ring to it. A terrified bureaucrat, probably childless, nothing to really lose but his own job, so his paranoia keeps him happy through the end of each week. His only moment of frailty is when he takes his Studebaker from the D.C. area to his home in Maryland to bring dinner to his mother. The radio along the way tranquilizes his anxiety the way scotch did for his boss and boss's boss—a perfect balance of fear and release. That is the man who would have written this:*

> The hard-fought security of the United States of America
> and its staunch allies is clearly being undermined by the
> excessive trust of defectors.

A patriot, that is what he would be—but something bigger: he believes in a moral world order where malevolent agents of Slavic and Sino origins are preparing to march through the capitol building and abolish the English language. He may not believe that this will happen, but he has imagined that it could happen, so it keeps him going:

Intelligence is not always reliable. To have any failure is a true tragedy, but they may be inevitable. However, there is reliable intelligence that Eastern European defectors from Soviet client states in the Soviet empire are doubling as Soviet agents for purposes of sabotage, espionage, and the reclamation or assassination of those who have defected before.

He's obsessed with the jargon and the realm. He thinks that if he talks about it enough, it will be less terrifying, like the true word for God. I bet he's a lonely one in a lazy way—the kind of guy who would give up country and someone else's king to the first Soviet spy that tried to fuck him. And I know why, even though this bastard never would. He is so weak that being faithful to whoever rules him is the best and all that he can do, the kind of guy who no one truly likes but that everyone is nice to in the way that tossing a dime to a homeless person is being nice. We have a few of those on the faculty.

Clearly, it is in the interest of the United States to curtail this obvious route of infiltration by the Soviet Empire.

Yes, the empire. I like that, because it actually was one. I like comparing America to an empire nowadays because humanity is too silly to resist the temptation of McDonald's. I wonder when McDonald's will appear in North Korea. More people have seen Ronald McDonald than have imagined the face of Mohammed. That is not empire; that is something else. Back to our little friend here of strong Protestant roots. Perhaps he could have been the son of a Daughter of the American Revolution if God had liked him a little more. Next life, my WASP-y little friend—next life.

In your next life your name will be Chappy, and you will play lacrosse, for it is the sport of the Northeast Indian tribes that is now unaffordable and undesirable to them. All this is fine because they will make your grandmother gamble away your inheritance in vulgar slot machines. You will major in political science after an adolescence of Tom Clancy and spy movies that you believe are real more than you believe in the reality of God. You will believe everything you hear from the government's lips because at your core you feel that the people in power deserve it. You will never travel because you will not see a reason to go past Lake Powell. You will never see that there is something wrong with people who crave power, for it is a moral baseness intellectually and spiritually beyond you. You see it all in terms of brilliant men making hard decisions, just as you should. You will retire in Maryland and tell stories to and about former colleagues and lacrosse players from those college days. Then you will die, and I pray for the city of New York that you are never created again—that your whiteness dies with you.

The Soviets have pre-empted this threat from democracy by blocking our agents seeking to join the communist political cause, but for the success of the patriot-then-traitor John Reed. It is not in the interests of the free world to allow this incessant tide of communist traitors to pollute the noble interests of the West.

We should be particularly weary of athletes from the Soviet client states of Ukraine, Czechoslovakia, Moldavia, Hungary, and East Germany. The well-documented Soviet prepping of their athletes with muscle-enhancing agents makes them prone to strict proselytization to the Soviet way of life. Some in this department assume that the pleasantries of a television and an apartment will make them reveal state secrets. This is highly unlikely considering the substantial cultural and emotional pull of Soviet influence. The communist renewal of . . .

Here his concentration could wane and large typos emerged accompanied by a looming smile on his face. He would type occasional words like Black and African and Master Rockefeller and conspiracy mixed with vowelless imitations of some obscure Slavic language, something that Uri could probably appreciate. When he reached the conclusion of his two-page treatise he smiled and removed it from the grip of the typewriter. Then he took out an enormous black marker and deeply inhaled its synthetically pleasing fumes before settling down to black out the Slavic words he had inserted. Then he went further into himself and blacked out random words from the beginning of the text: sometimes vowels, sometimes prepositions, just enough to make the dry text interesting through a kind of innuendo. He wondered if that is why certain words were blacked out so to make dry, boring government documents compelling. A black mark where a word once stood could mean the collapse of an empire or the murder of a person—anything. That mark encouraged historians to fill in the blank with their own view of how things always were.

Jerome was pleased, spiritually sated. Tomorrow he would present his class with xeroxed copies of government paranoia regarding the people, like Uri, sleeping in nothing but gray wool socks at the end of the hall. His students would be impressed, as well they should. Even after the Freedom of Information Act, it was still tricky to get documents that condemned the government so fluidly.

Mentioning the Rockefeller—that man had his paws into everything, another sack of flesh like all of us, but then again, he must have been something more. He would be again tomorrow when students were forced to contemplate what he had to do with the document placed before them.

Somewhere between mythical Rockefeller and slumbering Uri Slävøvic there was a bridge and a connection over the oceanic gap of history and moral bulwarks that separated their lives. Or perhaps they were strangers brought together by black, synthetic-smelling marker on a piece of paper chronicling conspiracies that must have existed but lacked the correct author to make them interesting and thus real. Jerome beheld his pages, noting the wonderful gaps between phrases, the poetic hatred and suspicion they evoked. Artists too frequently sold out to the beautiful and the controversial. To have a searing razor of doubt and contempt buried in one's soul . . . that was what the artist should be. That is the gift he should give to the world.

Michelangelo could never know me, Jerome thought, *and I guess I can never know him.* He placed the work in the shiny briefcase he used specifically for this occasion and gently laid it in the corner of the room, like a fetish on the altar of a dead religion. Jerome smiled at the muffled sound of Uri snoring in his new personal space. Then he looked in the mirror and wondered what was to be done with this new Slavic toy. Better than a teddy bear, this one should be the best white boy yet. His destiny would come to him in his sleep. He would conjure that one dream that would answer everything as it always had for all people who had ever lived.

Verse 4

The next day Jerome left the house to teach his class, without seeing Uri. He trusted Uri not to steal because he was certain that he would not know any better. Above Jerome's head, Formica halls buzzed with fluorescent lights as he entered his school. A power surge made him think paparazzi were waiting for him even though they never had been before.

As Uri was waking, Jerome was waving the original forgery he had created the night before in his hand. He decried the powers that had always been and certainly were now. Then he distributed xeroxed copies of his forgery to his students and told them to read it over. Every artist should have his moment of glory. This one felt like it could never end for it had always been baked into history. Yet it did, and then the lesson began.

He lectured about how the government had treated the inevitable human refuse of its empire as mere tools to further its ends. He expounded on the thesis that without the idea of treason there would be nothing to fight. Could the students imagine a political system in which the very concept of treason did not exist?

Their eyes understood, and Jerome saw the seed of a new batch of conscripted souls against the menace of the White.

On the third row of the class, second from the window, a student with taut, dusty skin delved deeper than all the others into the document in front of him. In that forgery he might have seen the true collapse of an empire. Perhaps he saw death by political monsters replaced with death by life. Maybe the paper became a blinding, glowing thing covered with black leeches that moved from word to word while revealing details in their wake.

The student decided it was his destiny to become a writer because in literature the details are everything while human life struggles and stumbles over its own manufactured routines. Utopia cannot exist when it is filled with people.

Uri slid across the floor in his socks. He had never been awake and naked for this amount of time in his entire remembered life. The room was a cramped rectangle. Within his confines he would slide and slide and slide.

His bladder took him away from his grand dance, so he begrudgingly put his clothes on and ventured into the hallway and gazed lopsidedly at the other rooms beyond his. The walls were barren, but for large slashes that upon his inspection revealed thousands of insects feasting on something Uri did not recognize.

He entered the bathroom and after a violent swoosh of water Uri looked at his disheveled hair over his disorganized face. Nothing seemed to be in the correct place. His eyes, those of a gentle wolf in another land, were timid to him.

Another reflection in another mirror behind him showed the ferocious Uri that had disembarked from a plane in a new land not twenty hours ago. That reflection then echoed off another wall and made a face that Uri found mysterious, like a child with a dangerous secret it had sworn not to tell. Uri reached his arm behind him to try to grab the reflection by his hair and demand information from it in Czech. But it did not say a word, always dodging just beyond the reach of his fingers before jumping across the room when Uri turned his head. Finally, he smiled and bowed to the victorious reflection that bowed back in return.

Straightening his mustache and longing for a hat, he left the bathroom and searched the house for Jerome. He watched the lazily moving pedestrians on the street and was amazed that no matter how hard he stared at them they refused to look back. When he stared at animals in a zoo they would look back and respond from their cages, but New Yorkers were different.

Jerome was presently giving a lecture on using a woman's body as a method of Cold War analysis. His hair turned ashen as he scribbled out irreducible proofs of his rightness on an expansive chalk board. Truths whose import faded into the dust of an eraser.

Jerome's class ended with a moment of inspiration for the fate of Uri. His destiny was inspired by an advertisement for Saint Patrick's Day Jerome had seen at the bar near campus for young alcoholics. A crimson grin emerged over his face as he remembered the ad:

"Everybody is Irish on St. Patrick's Day!"

Behind the text was a picture of a Chinese man in a leprechaun suit drinking a glass of green-tinted beer. The world of the white was always somewhat of a mystery to Jerome, and that's what he preferred.

The slow wait for the subway flicked at Jerome's mind as he frantically raced to compose the next document for his class. A title was missing. The worn, faint stench of a thousand commuting bodies fatigued him. Then the relief from the gust of air before the subway came. It both cooled and depressed him. He wanted to be at home by his enormous refrigerator, seated in a patent-leather office chair, occasionally looking up to know that he would never starve—a definite win he had over the rest of the world.

Then, the title for his next document emerged in his skull in steaming letters:

> Chronicling Attempted Acts of Tergiversation by Czecho-
> slovakian immigrants in the Boston Area.

White history had always fascinated Jerome. His favorite story was about William of Orange slaughtering the Irish of Green due to religion or some other pretense of violence. St. Patrick's Day was coming, and Jerome loved the fact that to this day in the richest nation to have ever existed the greens could still be enraged by the oranges. They didn't even understand why, like the drowning pressure of sin.

The whites that had branched off to the oranges were in need of a representative, someone for the silent, seething majority to cheer for as he soberly fights the good drunken fight.

Jerome and Uri walked across Madison Avenue and took a right at the first mannequin Uri saw. It was a giant woman of chrome flesh, wearing a flannel flying hat and scarf. Her body was enveloped in a blue and white uniform that Uri could not place. In front of her a real woman stood and almost reached out to her doppelgänger idol to shatter the hold of her lifeless stare.

Uri looked at the living woman and tried to place her. She was certainly not Czech. Her eyes conveyed a hardened innocence she shared with the mannequin. It seemed tragic that this plastic form of woman resembling metal was such an appealing thing to this woman with which Uri was rapidly falling in love. Behind her people quickly moved and Uri tried to take mental snapshots before it all left his life forever. Then he closed his eyes in a kind of prayer to make the photo last. When he opened his eyes the girl in front of the mannequin, the one he wanted to fall in love with, was gone.

He looked again to the mannequin and suddenly found her to be the most beautiful of all. She would never move—never be unfaithful except when she let her sleek, preened body be gawked at by anyone who cared to take the time to look. He gazed at her and felt for a muscle on his body that she seemed to have and that he knew he did not. She would never be his because she could not be anybody's and that was enough. Uri wondered if it was enough for everyone else, too.

Jerome started to become uncomfortable, and a visible wave of panic slapped him. Uri walked forward down a slight hill until he was in front of a cosmetic store. Inside stood a woman who glowed in his eyes. She looked far prettier than the customer she was helping. Uri could tell just by looking at the back of her skull. She looked like a girl he had seen in Prague a long time ago doing the same thing in an identical store but for a different colored marquee above the angel inside. He had stumbled upon a universal truth and he was not sure what it was. Something about light. The sterile lighting of these places demanded that the women inside be beautiful. It was the same uncomfortable light Uri had found in hospitals, the light that forced him to squint down the long corridors of phantasm sheets and doctors.

The light inside was too honest, so she had no choice but to be beautiful. Uri pitied her and thought she was like a captured and captive genius never able to sleep because of what it was. Down the street he saw the same things with different names repeating in an infinite, gentle slope that arched upwards to the point where Uri could no longer follow it.

The silver eyes of the woman dressed in cloth and chrome observed Uri as he looked at her and smiled, deeply bowing his head before he dashed into the cosmetic store and counted the lights above, at last picking the one that would end the rest. With a small leap and a long stretch of his arm he hopped and gently tapped the bulb with his callused fingers and shattered it into the form of a thousand shapeless angels that dusted his hair. Some of the other lights went to black, too.

She looked at him with visible confusion and seemed somewhat concerned that the thousand raining shards would penetrate his flesh. She tried to hide her concern. Grinning, he told her that his name is Uri, hoping she could see the smile under his mustache as he ran out the door to pursue Jerome.

Jerome sensed that Uri was committing a crime he could not quite name and had bolted.

Uri saw him sprinting away, and before Jerome's wind had exhausted itself, Uri grabbed him by the shoulder while keeping the same smile from before.

"Pretty fast for a white boy." He panted as they went into the cover of a subway station.

"I am not Whiteboy, I am Czechman." The breeze of the looming subway hit them again, and this time Uri detected a shiver around his throat before they entered the train. He tried to think of which direction they were going, but it did not matter because up above he could not see the sun. He only saw the skyscrapers illuminated by day.

"Ok, Czechman—or maybe Pragueboy would be better. What did you come here to do?"

"I tell you already. Adventure."

"Good, that is exactly what I am going to give you. We are going to the bus station now."

"I want to visit New York."

"You did. Breaking a white light in a store and looking at bitches buying clothes is New York. You don't want that tourist shit—Statue of Liberty, and all that. You can't visit New York; you have to live here, 'cause, let's face it, Europe might have us beaten with cobblestones and fine pussy on bicycles everywhere and old buildings where old white men died and signed shit, but New York has the best fucking people in the world. That is why they are here, because in some part of their skull they know that to be anywhere else would be a waste of their talents. Then of course these people need servants, so the city gives them cheap housing in Co-Op City. I actually will show you that place. It's where the bumbling motor that makes this place progress lives— the servant's quarters for the city. Everyone who cleans up shit or drives a machine they could never afford lives there. Quite impressive, really. That place will fuck you up; you really never been out of the Styx."

"I am from Prague; it is capital of Czech Republic."

"Right right right. Bet there's nothing in Czechoslovakia like Co-Op City. We're getting off here, and I'll show you something." The compulsion nagged to be a good host and to possibly expose Uri to the things that all visitors should see in New York besides newly born bagels and Disney Broadway productions.

A subway to a bus to a walk led them to the exterior of Co-Op City—stark because of its isolation and space. The bricks reddened with the rising day, and Uri felt the sun directly on his cheek through a miasmic, cigar-smoke haze. They looked like abandoned pillars from a factory outside of Prague he had never thought to remember until this moment. Uri touched one misshapen pentagon on the chain-link fence. He stared through the link in his hand to the third apartment from the right, the one on the twentieth floor; it felt small to him. It was the same apartment that Jerome watched so intently, although he knew no one who lived there. Jerome wished he had been born there so he could look back on his life with pride and astonishment at all he had overcome.

"I want to go to that apartment." Uri pointed to the one he had been looking at. Jerome glanced at his finger and, for reasons he could not explain, he knew exactly where he wanted to go, for it was where Jerome wished he had been born.

"You can't just go wherever you want, this ain't Prague. I'm sure they'd love to kill you, though, for asking."

"Why? I just want to see apartment."

"'Cause they don't have anything."

"They have apartment?"

Behind the normal din of traffic, a powerful bass tumbled through the atmosphere. A black car, waxed and preened, that Uri immediately identified as German and Jerome saw as foreign, drove behind them and next to another car, brown, humble, relatively new, American, which had been sitting there and watching.

The men exited the cars and tensely approached each other. Jerome restrained Uri, who effortlessly broke free and rushed over to the two cars, waving as he approached. The blue horizontal lines of his shirt might make him look fat from that distance.

"I see you," Uri said to the tallest, strongest member of the group. The tall, strong man lunged his head backwards, exposing his confused eyes shielded by the wide, black glasses that showed only the evil he wanted the world to expect from him.

The man turned his back on Co-Op City and approached Uri and shoved him in the chest. The force of the blow was barely detected. Uri shoved the man back in his chest and dropped him to the ground. He then said, "Hello!" and that it was nice to finally meet all of them. The man on the ground stood up too slowly, and the entire group was now laughing. It was another scene that had been repeated before in their youths and in their mothers' eyes.

"Finally, I meet you. I see you all the time on Music Television in Prague."

They laughed, slowly and with staccato.

"Where you from, Opie?" The one that had pushed Uri and fallen as a result turned out to be partially deaf, and beyond this he admitted a profound difficulty hearing the dialects of others, particularly the Whiteman.

"I am from Prague; it is in Czech Republic."

"What the hell a lil Opie like you doing here?" Uri looked confusedly to the leader of the gang for a translation.

"Why are you here, young grasshopper?"

"Ah yes, of course, I was expecting the freestyling. I am here for adventure." He smiled as he spoke.

"Adventure—your ass flew all the way from wherever to come to the Co-Op."

"From Prague," he rolled his r's like his mother said his first father did. "And yes, I am here now."

"And you saw us on Prague 1 Music Television—Sonny-Bono-save-the-zebras-then-the-Africans-whatever network."

"No, I saw you on Music Television."

"Really." His cheeks smiled while the rest of his face did not. "You hear that, fellahs? The Co-Op Hill Gang just got big in wherever."

"'Bout mothafucking time," a voice from the chorus croaked.

"What's your favorite track, yo?" The leader stared into Uri. Beneath the coveralls and blue-striped shirt both men were the same, but the leader had seen more women naked and somehow both knew it.

"I do not know the English word. There was only Czech subtitles on the bottom. But very good." Uri began to hum the vibrant beat of the hip hop he had heard what felt like another lifetime ago. Gradually, it faded to black in his mouth as the jumbled current of English words lost their flow.

The sonorous bass from the belly of the black car raised its voice, compelled by an unseen hand—a thumping beyond his experience in Uri's chest that he quickly learned to love. Together they all listened. The rest of the gang nodded their heads in rhythmic agreement while the bass from the car mysteriously rose in volume and compelled Uri's torso to sway back and forth as a cobra's metronome. Nothing could be understood by Uri but for the rhythm, that force that blended with his body. His ears perked away from the motion of his head when a line he remembered emerged. ". . . I be in Prague cashing niggaz like they was a Czech."

Uri stopped and smiled, placing a closed fist next to this head, palm facing outwards. He held it there in a type of Slavic salute they had never seen before but understood completely. Then in one swift motion he shot his fist down in front of his solar plexus like a boxer gloating over his fallen adversary or a childhood friend.

Uri turned abruptly and departed back to an astonished Jerome, who followed him as they walked away together on crisp dead grass. The sound of the bass was subsumed by passing traffic. Jerome asked Uri what that gesture meant, and Uri responded that it was his gesture and that he would give it to Americans that he felt deserved it. Since he did not have money he would give them something far more valuable.

The walk to the subway station was long, and Jerome hesitated before sending Uri away. He was drawn to the blue stripes hugging his body like an abstract painting one could later not describe. He noted the colors again and that they had to be replaced with a vibrant orange shirt for his trip to southern Boston for his celebration of St. Patrick's Day.

Jerome needed a martyr for his great cause, and it was at the tender moment before they submerged under the city again to ride the subway to his departure that Jerome Ironside felt a divine hand had sent Uri to him to complete this great mission. Why else would he have possibly arrived at the bus station and appeared under the light of Jerome's waiting eyes?

Jerome treated Uri to dinner at a small, terrible place before sending him to his hopeful demise on St. Patrick's Day in Boston. Uri told him over the meal how his life had been extremely hard and soft.

Jerome understood.

Jerome was sending Uri to the address of a former student of his, the only other person who understood. Uri would sleep there for a few hours before being set free in the city, fatigued and confused. It would be as Jerome instructed when he called his former student for the first time in two years while Uri was riding through the claustrophobic forests of Connecticut.

At the bus station Jerome led Uri by his wrist like a child and placed him in front of where he needed to be to do what Jerome wanted in the world. People shouldered by Uri with a lazy rudeness that moved him further onto the bus until at last Jerome looked one last time and tilted his head and walked away, joining the exodus crowd from the station.

Jerome descended to the subway and, for the first time, felt himself in the belly of a benevolent serpent fueling the glorious mass above. Each soul up there resonated within him, playing its own ephemeral and discordant tune that left only truth in its wake. He imagined himself ascending above the city until all he could see was motion. Then he would stop and feel its discordance, appreciating every dialect formed within a single street and generation, every pang of loneliness from the long-time resident stranger in his own home. Then the bliss from those who had formed roots, fissures in the surface of the world deeper than culture, an expanding life beyond the pages of imagination—the color of another culture for him to envy from his accession. He was different from the others, he knew this. He had to leave that great home below in order to understand it.

By the time the subway had passed him by, he was ascending the stairs towards his familiar home. His euphoria had fled. The new stasis of life without Uri gave him his direction again, and he wanted to return home before the city lit up with the lights of man so the evening sun could kiss the off-white page on his typewriter before he took the marker to slash out the history he was creating that had probably been. History would continue to be created tomorrow for his class and for Uri on his first day in Boston. It was St. Patrick's Day when all the whites would cower under lagers of green, perhaps indulging enough to have opportunities to propagate their vile species. Uri was the spark to a key to the heart of white America's tender weakness. In Uri we should trust.

Verse 5

U ri's bus entered Boston on a taught St. Patrick's Day morn with air that felt stretched over his face. The barely slumbering Bostonians had not yet emerged for their revelry. Uri smiled. The great surge of expectancy spurted in his stomach while his frazzled mustache grumbled for sleep. An odor of unexpected human origin wafted from the scratched metal lining of the bus, a kind of cleansing sage sanctifying each traveler that made this journey from the humming nights of New York to the granite mornings of Boston. Then there were those bound for the more southern-American climes, where the latitude stretched with the bellies of the people. Uri would never see the equator before he died his fantastic death, but he would always imagine it.

As the bus shifted into a higher gear he saw a globe on a halogen-illuminated billboard and imagined it being a torso. Small limbs peaked through its crust like the snout of a newly born reptile. Within the world's chortling interior were representatives of different cultures from around the world. All of them danced: the tall and broad amongst the supple and lean.

The image remained in Uri's mind after the billboard passed and occupied him until his mustache became jealous and pricked him slightly, demanding to be smoothed back into place. Then another billboard of fading luminance emerged. Passing him and distracting him. His eyes languorously closed and opened again when the bus had ceased from motion, and it was his time. Off he went, sniffing his clothes and remembering the journey from moments before.

Uri started to doubt his decision to leave his luggage behind with Jerome even though he believed in the American myth that those who arrive with the least would receive the most. Still, the smell on his clothes lingered no matter how quickly he walked to elude it.

As Uri strolled along he remembered a smokestack that blended seamlessly with Prague's numbing winters. He sniffed the new smells while passing the man who was sent by Jerome to fetch him. The man had to look away from the nearly blinding orange of Uri's shirt. He thought that Jerome's art had nearly reached its conclusion and that he should be just about be ready to die as he had wanted.

The man behind Uri hesitated to touch him. The color seemed too bright and obscene. He had lived in Boston for almost his entire life and the cultural memory of the city told him that this was wrong. A severe thing had been done. It was only the faith in Jerome's mental superiority that compelled the observer's hand to touch Uri on the shoulder and bring him away to his rattling car.

Inside the car the conversation spewed out in a rapid, rifle staccato.

"I am Uri, what is your name?"

"Doesn't matter, you're jus chillin' at my place for a few hours."

"Oh, thank you for your hospitality."

"Mmm."

"I am from Prague."

"Mmm."

"I like American life, I like New York."

"Uh-huh."

Uri paused, he read the list of greetings he had in his mind, frustrated that English was not fluid like water but an unending act of memorization. "Fuck Osama Bin Laden."

The driver of the car smiled.

"That's all right, you're an OK cat, tell you what's going to happen, we'll take a little nap at my pad, and then there is a party outside of the house. You're gonna go outside in that orange Sunday best, and then Jerome will be a happy man, and I don't have to think about him anymore."

"I like Jerome, he is the only American without a car."

The driver snorted without laughing. "I don't want to be rude, but could you stop talking, I need to concentrate on the road."

"Certainly, I just wanted to express my sincere gratitude."

"What country did you learn English in, London, or one of its baby-daddy colonies."

"I learned it in Berlitz."

"Where is that?"

"Prague."

The car was silent for the remainder of the trip while a moist fog condensed over the passing lights above until they reached the house. Two floors shared by four people and each with his own room. The driver pointed Uri to his bed and then slept on the couch in the front of the house. Closing his eyes while feeling the relief that he would never have to speak to Jerome again. Before he welcomed a heavy sleep he thought of that poor honkey a floor above, the original bohunk. A new sacrifice. One individual can make a difference. He believed that much. Still, Jerome never understood even that. Jesus was killed, Lincoln was shot, people disagree, but this creature creakily sleeping a floor above was not of myth. He was his own kind of extraordinary. The father should give something more to the son than martyrdom or glory. He should also give more than he is capable.

Uri slept upstairs. His keeper below. Outside the streets barely churned, expecting.

Mid-morning light rested on Uri's face and tickled his eyes and mustache before he chose to wake, rested. He sneezed and his eyes blasted open.

The room was painted black with a writing desk that had no chair. Uri saw a door and opened it and found a closet full of literature and scattered clothing and tapes for learning languages he had never heard spoken. He thought that if Berlitz did not know it neither should he. He pulled his coveralls over his glowing orange shirt and marveled at the comfort of the fabric, then went downstairs hungry.

The driver sat at a table, anxious to get Uri out before his housemates awoke. His home was near a monolithic cluster of bars and sometimes the driver would sit on his roof, concealed like a sniper, and watch the giddy degeneracy while flipping through a novelty deck of cards containing pictures of starving children in Africa and the telephone number to adopt them. The pack was several years old, and the box they came in stolen by a friend. Statistically, most of these kids should be dead. He liked holding the cards and believing that their last chance was in his hands. Before puberty he had learned magic, and with the cards, he would refresh his memory of sleight of hand moves.

Then he would look back at the streets below and afar and longingly hope to see an assault, not a rape, but an assault. To watch the weak, liberated by numbers and emboldened by booze, have their day to find someone stronger, a powerful innocent to provoke and pummel in oblivious rage. Then they would change the story of what happened on that day. Yet the observer, the driver, had seen it all. His mind knew. The deck of cards drew sweat away from his excited hand.

Still, before the driver's vision of destiny could occur, Uri had to eat. He slid a basket of bread and a bottle of blood red wine to Uri. The driver thought of the last time he had eaten every possible bite of food like Uri was doing now. It was the last time he had known true hunger and then the memory plunged back below. After all of the bread had been consumed Uri drank the wine in parakeet gulps while rapidly tilting the bottle before he leaned back, sated and ecstatic, and asked his host if the wine was from Moravia.

"You know I never betrayed you." The driver's voice was solemn and apologetic.

Uri thought he was not being a good guest, so he squished his enormous frame inwards to become smaller and take up less room.

"Pardon me."

"I never betrayed you, you know that?"

Uri scanned the sentence and then thanked him heartily for his hospitality, asking the man where he was supposed to go next.

"Outside, everyone is drunk, it should be fun." The host stretched his neck towards the ceiling. Uri asked him if he was going too and the man said no, that he did not drink, so why bother talking to people under the spell of oblivion.

Uri felt that it was time to leave and shook the man's hand before going outside into an urban valley of St. Patrick's Day in a tide of green. He stood on the porch and proclaimed himself the new king of this town. Boston, that was the name. The sun was shining. It was a regal day indeed. Time to grab life by the hand and shake it.

Most of the bars had not yet opened, but still the men seethed with anticipation while back home the women prepared for work or to join them later. The morning pint of Guiness had slithered to their stomach and inspired a declaration of love for the brew and then a gritty lamentation that it was better in Ireland and that there was something wrong with the American way that gave them the city of Boston.

To drink the blood of the homeland is to drink a tradition, a history with integrity. Uri looked at the unsmiling faces and thought that the Irish and Czechs really had almost everything in common except language. They were middle children nations. Incessantly occupied, raked and razed through the ambitions of another land, another culture, but in the end implacable. The Czechs knew the nature of this and wondered why the Irish had bothered to capture Boston.

Uri smiled at this American version of an aged European king-
dom. There was still some middle child left in this place. His traveler's
shadow reminded him that America was not capable of destroying
the humiliations and angst of history. There can be guilt in life simply for just being. A culture's memory is the most inaccurate and
unforgiving of them all.

He thought that the European knows as little about history as the
American does about remembrance. They are names given to other
devices and in the beauty of their incomprehensibility their fates are
tied. Two enormous islands on the globe that cannot be torn apart.

Uri walked until he found a bench in a causeway that he pre-
dicted would soon be full of people. His mustache fluttered with
worry but he decided to veto its concern. Everything was too fresh to
be subjected to instinct, still the muddy sentiments of dread loomed.
Dread was always something he connected to the middle child. Uri
felt the scratch of his psychological suit and thought of his family.
He sat down staring at the people ahead of him who stared back and
pointed, whispering threats about him to themselves over the din of
the morning bar. When the drunken hunger of the afternoon would
take control, they would find that sack of flesh from Prague wearing
orange and sitting contentedly and then they would destroy him like
the drink devours memory.

Uri bathed in his contentment and the knowledge that he had
made the correct decision to leave all he knew behind. He was a
baby constantly reborn but for his short hair and bushy mustache
veiling his always-blooming innocence. This was now a nation of
first-borns and that is why the Irish here felt the way they did. It was
a sensation that Uri knew and could only articulate now, on a bench,
in a bright orange shirt, on a spotless day in Boston.

The trickle of people gradually increased to a stream. Uri sat
at the precipice to a row of bars a block away all bearing the flag

of the Irish tribe. He became the beacon for a thousand insults and the cackling of victorious strangers, euphoric, incapable of remembering.

The driver lay still atop his perch. Motionless but for his gentle breathing and slow strokes of the cards in his hand. Unbeknownst to the driver others were watching as well. One of them gazed at Uri from under a large Nazi flag that covered his wall but that was shielded from the gaze of outsiders who bothered to look. Yet, it was always there protecting him and compelling him forward.

He stared at Uri in awe for he saw another just like him. Another who must have hated as he hated. Someone else devoted to the destruction of the white race. He stroked the pale, scruffy skin atop his head and looked at his reflection in the glass of a framed picture of his fifth-grade class. There were exactly 100 students. Statistically, some of them should be dead or have dropped out of school, or committed rapes, or been raped. Maybe 3 or 4 out of 10. He ran his finger along every white face and counted, hoped, and prayed for the sake of the few and the destruction of all.

Somewhere else, someone else was running his finger over the same picture.

Now in his twenty-second year, Clive McDermott lifted his finger from the photo and looked at his shone head that would never shine and wondered why it had all happened like this. He had written a paper once condemning white culture for every evil in the world. He received an F and the contempt of his teacher, but it was the most rewarding grade of his life for in that well-researched secondary-school document he had uncovered a truth that made an educated man enraged.

Oblivious and excited, Uri stood with his back to the flags of Ireland. He had met a teacher from the Isle of Mann in Prague and wondered if any of these people knew him. They seemed so close but maybe were as different as he and the Moravian mafia members he had borrowed some money from after meeting them in a bar once upon a time.

The thick orange pigment on his shirt drew sweat from his skin and he crossed his arm across his brow as if cleaning a freshly used knife and then looked at the fabric to see that it had darkened. Orange was not a color that should be dark. Through the window of a tavern across the street several large Americans soaked themselves in pints of Guinness and glared at Uri. He had become an itch in the morning that demanded to be scratched.

The sun cast its rays down and ascended. Beneath the light the taverns, pubs, and bars, whose differences in meaning Uri did not know, absorbed people from the street. Uri felt like the light was trying to bake him and because of this and his curiosity, he waited. His skin began to feel like it was in an oven, so he waited further still. In the bars an impulse of communal violence hit the crowd the way euphoria does a junky's mind as the plunger depresses almost into his vein.

They stared at Uri in his bright orange shirt like frothing moths before a suicidal flame. The whimsical bartender that dispensed sardonic advice every day to his regulars, closer to them now than the priests ever since the scandals, growled before noting that the man in orange must be the only guy in the world to have missed the commercial that everyone is Irish on this day. His words streamed out in a fusion and a fury straight from the Old World through his DNA. His rage, his language, his poetry. Words a great grandfather had said once that had never again been uttered until now. The barman remembered this and something else and vowed to physically return to the land of his ancestors to spend the rest of his days by next autumn.

The sentiment of booze channeled from the others into him. Every friend whose jaw had been broken or black-eyed wife or whisky-lusted teenager bubbled within him. He had never been of import in the way television made him want to be. He knew he was a tapestry that the community was painted upon. Green and white, and when the barman so willed it, moments of sloshing blood red.

The barman abstained from alcohol until moments like this traipsed upon him once a decade. His men, his troops, were staggering on their stools and eager to do something, and the strange man in the orange shirt with the coveralls wearing a mysterious mustache was alone. Too foreign to speak to. Something of the strange man needed to be destroyed and its shards hurled all the way back to the Old World.

The barman became taller and slammed the bell above his head and most eyes found him while some drifted away. He raised his bar towel as a battle flag and passionately spoke of a man named O'Shane who had died senselessly but was remembered well. The men knew this and nodded. Then the barman spoke about funny

things that O'Shane had said in life and a patron muttered something about him being the best goddamn . . . something, the exple-
tives expressed the emotion and everyone chuckled. Nothing made
sense but everything was understood.

The barman thanked the old man and affectionately called him
Scotty then Boy-o. He then spoke of the tradition of the neighborhood, everyone was here, so the silent skinny one in the back who
always had two jobs he hated locked the door for this moment
to prevent any neighborhood tourists from entering. He looked to
the barman and he nodded back with a gentle smile. He poured
a round of Jameson whiskey while talking about his evil and hapless father whom he loved now more ardently than he had ever
before because he was dead. They toasted their fathers and sipped
and swallowed. Enjoying the fumes as they exited their nostrils
while leaving a pleasant burn behind. He looked again at Uri while
speaking of their tradition on this day and their gazes followed,
no one knew him. Each breath he took was a desecration of the
memories of their ancestors. The bartender spoke of the bench
Uri sat on and the memories he had there. The orange emanating
from Uri pricked the bubble of their communal thoughts and all
of their heads began to flood with rage. He implored the skinny
man in the back to unlock the door and he did. Then everyone in
the bar stood as a pool of water without a limit, released when the
barman nodded his head and the wave of rage crashed onto the
street. The chatty men went first followed by the violent ones that
felt surges of strength from a thousand generations that had lived,
suffered, and perished in far greater ways than what was about to
happen to the man in orange.

"Hello friends, my name is Uri, and I am from Prague."

A voice came into coherent focus, harsh and intonated, "Is everyone in Prague that fucking ugly bitch?" Uri looked to see where the voice came from and then realized that all these Americans looked the same as they swayed together with furrowed and glazed eyes. Out of deference for cultural differences, Uri pretended not to understand or take offense. He knew what the word fuck meant, he had looked it up once after watching *Easy Rider*, but it did not fit in his life now. He continued to smile.

"So where is the party today?" Uri spoke and the crowd leaned back as if fazed and wounded.

"Right here, you fuck." There was that word again. He thought about it, but it did not make sense. Something was wrong with their English.

From behind the crowd a cop emerged, slowly, moving through the growing swell of angry and curious spectators until he arrived at the eye of the storm. Uri had a clearance of one of his body lengths that no one had violated until the cop stood in front of him and looked down, squinting in disbelief and rage.

"What are you doing?" His freckled fingers tapped out of rhythm on his night stick. Behind the cop and behind the crowd more people were joining to observe what they could not see. Strangers from other bars caught in the gravity of the moment.

"I am doing nothing; I am talking to my new friends." The cop's eyes looked askance at the crowd. They looked back with hope as children will whose parents are about to release them into an arcade.

"New friends, huh. You Irish by any chance?" Suddenly the cop's speech slipped into the accent of his father. Sometimes it happened during moments like this when he absolutely knew that the men beside him had the same values. An unspoken trust between brothers going back to the Old World.

"I am not Irish; I am from Prague."

"Another European fuck come to Boston, well, on behalf of the city let me welcome you here." The cop's fingers stopped moving and he turned to the crowd and asked them what time it was. Several people groggily looked at their watches and then replied that it was half-past ten. "Early enough to have a few spirits, eh fellas." They smiled and he grimaced back. The cop moved beside the ear of the biggest one, the man in front who was the leader for this reason and told him that it was early enough, don't kill him, but make sure he understands the meaning of the Irish for the rest of his life. The large man smiled, and the cop nodded.

When the cop exited the shield around Uri burst and the crowd surrounded him. The man closest grabbed him by his collar and smashed his hand into Uri's cheek bone. The blow stung Uri. He then raised his hand to his face and wiped the pain away and then felt better. He was not sure what had happened.

Uri looked up to the sky and with whimsy noted falling stones and pieces of lumber pirouetting towards him. Perhaps also a bird that had died too young and in flight. An enraged small man ran towards Uri and kicked him in the shins as hard as he could like he was at a carnival game with an important prize at stake. He was aiming for Uri's genitals.

The crowd engulfed Uri all pushing each other from the back until he was surrounded in a miasma of flesh struggling within itself.

Uri did not understand what was happening, but apparently one of his two observers did. When the cop had first approached the mass of men Clive McDermott had seen what was to be and started to race down with a baseball bat ready to protect the things that Uri represented to him.

The violence was like a slow magnetic force that slowly drained the bars of men who stood like pack prey on the Serengeti straining their necks and ears to ascertain what they could not see.

The cop again emerged and smiled at the newcomers as he had smiled at the large man in the circle before him. Smiling and nodding, once again he walked down the street and turned away to leave the scene of a crime he did not commit yet had created. One of his powers that gave him great satisfaction. Uri became protected from the assaults in the front as fighting emerged in the back and the bodies pressed onward tumbling and growling and struggling. From his rooftop, the driver watched it all and then riffled his cards into the air, astonished.

"Well, Jerome, Mr. Ironside, here is your martyr, and this is your moment, I think that the cameras might miss this one, but they missed Jesus, too, so don't worry. Look at them go, it's incredible. You'll never understand these people, Jerome, like I do, but I chose not to believe that it's all true, that is my way, and my debt to you is finished. Paid."

With tepid disinterest the driver looked at the melee focusing on the center where Uri should be as the flow of the conflict moved away from the bench and took on its own growth and nature. Waxing and waning, a season of carnage and decay in an instant. Then the mass of flesh and violence moved away down the street revealing Uri who was calmly sitting with a bright red cheek. If the driver had not just seen what he had seen he would have thought Uri was just another drunk honkey.

A shiny flash of white skin emerged from the now empty periphery and heroically grabbed Uri from the bench. Bald flesh glistened in the morning. It looked young. It could have been a child as things without hair can be timeless. He pulled Uri to his feet and the driver watched his lips move. It was identical to a war film. Uri looked at the hand tugging his orange shirt and shrugged. Then he stood up and slowly followed the excited bald head running to his house. His steps were short, frantic, and jangled while pulling Uri in psychological tow across a scorched morning sun that reflected off the face of his driver and passive attempted murderer. Meanwhile, the brawl disintegrated down the street because it was starting to become personal between the whites.

Verse 6

*C*live McDermott beckoned Uri in through the front door while shushing him with the middle finger of his other hand. When Uri entered the house Clive McDermott pointed to his gently snoring mother in front of a muted television.

Uri was taken into another room and then stood in front of the flag bearing a swastika that was displayed the way a statue of a martyr would be at a church altar.

"What do you think yo, you like dat shit, you like man?" Clive's voice was jittery with a rhythm all his own that Uri could not understand so he faked it and smiled. "Shits like steel, y'know, the whole fucking thing is coming down."

Uri thought of one of his probable fathers his mother had told him about. He was a German who did nothing during the war and that the Czechs then expelled from his own country. He and Uri's mother did not like each other anyway so war provided the best reason for divorce. It is always easier to believe that someone is dead than to deal with the living entity that absorbs so much natural hate. This swastika was not his father, but it was German and definitely not Irish.

"What is this thing?" Uri pointed for clarity. "It does not belong here."

"Fuck man, what're you talkin'? Course it blongs here, this shit here, biggrn Hitler, biggrn you, gonna bring the whole fucking thing down, da race, everything man, all comin down."

Uri blinked slowly and twitched his mustache before speaking again. "Have you heard of Berlitz company? Perhaps you could take their classes. They have excellent instructors."

Clive twitched his nose in confusion. "I dunno what da fuck you saying. Don't you see man? We the same, same souljahs in this war, all of it coming, raining white every day until dawn. It's da fuckin war of the century, only few people know about it."

"The war on terrorism is well known. People in Prague remember September 11th very well."

"Fuck that! All propaganda, quit fuckin wit me. I got to show you the shit. You know what the fuck is up wearing that shirt today. We in a war, and we gonna win, a race war, bringing down the white man, these cracker bohunk beer swillin babies fucked the whole world up, this thing, this whiteness, this white-o city needs to die."

Uri pulled one of his sleeves up and sat and listened while the smooth white flesh of the talking head moved its vibrant pink lips in front of him.

Clive stopped speaking, stood up, and moved his turntables underneath the swastika flag. Almost in prayer he put one ear in a headphone and the other attached to some outside world. He looked at Uri while switching records and went over to sit beside him and spoke in words he thought he would understand. "Look, look at the world today. What is the problem with it? Disease everywhere, people starving every year, it's not even a problem now, nothing big, just the culture of Africa, I send my apologies from God, but you people are damned, not your fault, must be God, I don't believe in God, so not my fault either. But you know something, you something big, it is someone's fault, not of a man, or a race, or a God, or a terrorist, but of this white thing. This culture that came to America and gave a disease it could not take back and never wanted to, God's sin was not placing us further apart. Those fucking ships should never have hit Haiti, they should have fallen off the side of the world like the European maps said. Then what did this culture do after that, do you know?"

Uri looked to the ceiling and saw a poster of a modern martyr who had found religion too late. Uri was not sure where and thought that maybe it was Asia.

"What's your name?"

Startled Uri looked into the intense eyes of his only American friend. "Jiři Slävøvic," he said.

"What?"

"I mean to say Uri Slavovic."

"Oh, cool, I'm Clive—Clive Duncan McDermott. So, listen, Uri. What does the white do after it comes to this place, goes to Africa and fucks them up even more. Turning themselves against each other to enslave the masses. I bet they didn't even know what race was back then, I bet it did not even exist until the white man came and gave it to them, another present, the only one not attached to the end of a white dick. Fuck man, I read all about it, they killed in Africa, they warred, they did all things human. But they never thought of a system to sell their own flesh, never had an identity other than birth. That was the white man's gift to them, a new identity, one of subservience, then of victim of God, too much for the white to take."

"I understand."

Clive ducked his head away from Uri like a jittery boxer.

"Oh yeah, when you look at that flag what do you see?"

Uri paused and reflected. The flag stood before a turntable while two burning candles sent tendrils of smoke into the air like new-born silk from a black widow. Outside the revelers were singing and wailing. The same men that had fought moments ago now sang for nothing. They had not forgotten the events surrounding Uri, but they did not care.

"You know what I see? Do you really want to know? I see the culmination of the white. I see every color that rose above transparency pushed back down. I see the potential to complete one thing that has not ended. They always say that the Nazis were defeated, that's more shit from the white, the Nazis weren't defeated, the Nazis are the white, they're just honest about it. Germany was defeated, destroyed, but Germany spread something through the world, took whiteness to the next level, made the system of whiteness real, codified the shit. Before Germany brutality, genocide, all that, just was an idea, a breach in civility, sure you could kill the others, but the whites had their own code. Then this beautiful swastika came in and took it to higher ground, the whiteness showed its way to the world, the system of white was born. You understand?"

Uri looked through the swastika, the symbol he could see spinning into eternity, four mad hatters holding onto the sides and rolling to oblivion. Or maybe it was the oblivion of the observer who watched them roll away.

"I understand," he said with solemnity.

"I know you do. Look what the fuck happened after Germany went away and the Nazis died, shit went down in Russia, Stalin fucked up all his cats, China same thing, how many millions dead, more than a tragedy, more than art can ever know. It's all the white, it changes people, every person it touches melts, becomes something new. Something white, the Nazis weren't destroyed, Germany bounced up again, higher than it had ever been. Then the white set its eyes on the world, and now it has it."

Uri stared at the swastika again and bowed his head before the flag. He felt something new, the sorrow of his companion, the half-truth of his life and the disgust of a thousand babies echoing from a neglected orphanage. He thought about times before in his life when he wished to die and wanted to kill.

There it all was under a flag with a turntable. A world order Uri had never thought of but always tasted. Something white, something in him, his culture or someone else's, Europe is a small place, not big enough for this but maybe it was of this. He stared at Clive's picture from elementary school and saw the faces of his own companions from elementary school. In another time what would they have been? The marcher of Jews, the pragmatic chemist, the adventurous conqueror of Africa, the band leader for the parade. They would have been all these things and he would never have condemned them because they were born of him. That same substance that made him Czech or Hungarian or from somewhere further east.

"We souljahs, y'know, this is our war, time to bring the bitch down, sumthin new for the masses, fuck the next generation, now is the time, before we all infected, before anything else gold gets turned to dust, this is our war." Clive placed his hand on Uri's shoulder and Uri reciprocated kindly and gently. Whispering so that only the picture and Clive could hear.

"I do not want to fight. I am from Prague." Uri's voice was strained and confused. He did not know what to do or think, only that every moment should receive his full enthusiasm. It was a promise he knew he could keep with this new land licking its way into his rapidly beating heart.

"C'mon, let's ride. I want to show you to my beautiful baby, then we hit up down south, show you what created you. The whole world bloomed from the seed of a civil war; you know that? Everything you are, everything you hate is from America, the South to be more precise. Jews gave us Jesus, Greeks gave us dem-o-crac-ey, Germans gave us Protestants, French gave us revolution, then America gave us hate. The grand telos, and it all went down in The South. But first you must meet my Nubian queen, the reason you should take a breath every day and I should be out there livin' the struggle."

Clive grabbed Uri by the shoulder and he followed. When he crossed the threshold of the doorway his mother roused. She sensed something in him and her pupils exploded under the cover of her dreaming lids.

"Clliiiiveee." Her voice crescendoed with the wood beneath as she sat forward. He paused at the door and led Uri outside while handing him the keys and his bag and then returned inside to finish the discussion his mother had begun with him in her shallow dream. Alone and outside under a gray St. Patrick's Day sun Uri smiled as he listened to Clive's mother lecture him on the nature of hard work.

He had car keys in his hand and was one act of theft away from becoming a true American with the freedom to travel west as far as he pleased. With keys, clothes, and a car he would become something more than he had ever been. Not only having more, but somehow, he would be more. A hungry European running from a stale past to an exciting present. Wind and music in his ears, hearing the coughing gentle secrets from the midnight sun for him and him only as he had earned it. The adventure was his and life's end had never been clearer: a crashing California wave coming down on the dream life of American bliss. It all stood as still as his heart before the next wave of blood went crashing down his chest. Clive patted him on the shoulder and took back his car keys and reminded Uri that in America we drive on the right side of the road so he had better be careful.

Uri entered the car and Clive instructed him how to fasten his seatbelt the way one would to a child. Then he spoke of the untold beauty and passion of his Nubian queen, something Europe and Uri could never know because they did not have the soul for it. That was the gift of These United States, a soul, a bright shining soul tattooed across the sky.

Clive McDermott saw it in the shimmering eyes of stretching skyscrapers in New York City, in Boston when the gentle flags waved across the Atlantic to Italy and Ireland, and in the bright white teeth of his ecstatic girlfriend when she arched her back towards God while her legs were spread over him. In that, their greatest moment together, he would rub his pasty, powerless hands over her slow-motion breasts and then extend them to the precipice of her quivering lips when she told him that he fucked good for a whiteboy.

Verse 7

Steadily and angrily Clive steered across an ascending freeway that rose shoulder to shoulder with stubby office buildings. They were masked and lusterless in the crepuscular moment of quiet that made Boston shine for a few minutes each day. Stalled traffic rushed towards him so he accelerated before tapping the brakes smoothly and quickly. He asked Uri if he could feel the power in the car before telling him that it was MC Clive McDermott that had added the energy he felt in his body. Uri smiled gently with his wolf eyes towards his new American friend. The look extended out the window and into the building behind the car where it caught the eye of an office manager, medium-sized and insecure, overlooking a sea of artists he had captured in cubicles so that they could create advertising campaigns season after season and year after year. The manager was certain that someday the soul of all these artists would be his. It was his destiny because it is what he prayed for in church every Sunday.

Under the manager's elevated office, the artists toiled to make a car as appetizing as the hamburger they had enhanced the week before. There was something still in them that connected to the adolescents they were in high school when they doodled pictures of their teacher and bug-eyed cats and mushrooms in the margins of class notes on American history. A year-long catalogue of the things that made this country and the people in it so wonderful with an occasional asterisk of the racial policies that impoverished the classes of people it did not exterminate.

The notebooks full of history and art would be buried in trash-cans or burned for the sake of youthful tradition. The doodles remained, though, indelible, and full of color in the memory of the artist's eye. The white cubicle people sat and labored with the knowledge that they were artists, that the cubicle and the medium-sized office manager sometimes snorting down their necks could do nothing to erode their identity. They were artists for the man but artists until the end. Something those poor commuter cattle on the highway out the window could never know.

The office manager looked back directly into Uri's eyes and told him exactly what was going on, the feeling of the life he had to endure in this constant wading of creatives. He would be richer than his father. This he knew.

Uri understood it all and then looked forward.

Clive accelerated away from the buildings and office managers and artists through the haze of humanity and into the emerging night. He pulled off the freeway when Uri began to feel dizzy and disoriented as he had lost the last landmark of a colonial mast on a ship in the harbor. Uri sat somewhere between astonishment and envy. He was exhausted and happy that another day had expired with his being nowhere near Europe or the legacy of his second father.

It was just past dusk when Clive and Uri arrived at Giovanne's Pizzeria. They had not traveled far but it had taken hours to navigate through the steel pollution. The pizzeria's awning was covered by a large cartoon rendition of a middle-aged Italian man stroking his mustache and presenting his giant pepperoni pizza to the dusty Boston night. Over his shoulder there was a flagpole where a dirty Italian flag limply flapped.

Next door to Giovanne's was a three-story house that seemed squeezed into the neighborhood. It looked identical to every other squeezed house except this one held two dusty draped flags: one Irish and one Italian. Uri paused for a moment to compare the flags from the two countries as Clive opened the door and released a strong whiff of cheese, dough, and humanity into Uri's nostrils. He twitched his mustache to relieve himself of the smell but to no avail. The blast of odor had left its essence in those robust whiskers, it was not going to leave. Again, he looked at the two flags. He thought about the difference in color between them. His mother had told him that his first father had been both of these things so they must be a part of him in this land. He would be happy to order a pizza although the throbbing soreness on his face from the morning's violence had made him drift considerably from his new Irish-American heritage. It felt too belligerent without a right to be. This rage had chipped the world into a smooth obsidian point that America wielded like a paint brush. With such violence where could there be grief except in a cultural memory and how could such a thing exist outside of the petty viscera of man?

Uri had learned these things from the Czechs. They were a small tribe in Eastern Europe, yet they existed still. Extrapolating their history from the uniqueness of their language. They knew they were ancient because so was the language. It was a cultural fact, greater than any stone tablet to a tribe wandering through deserts of infinite wind.

Uri wondered how there can be a creation story without a language? A culture's language should be born before its God.

Clive fully opened the door and released the fluorescent hue of the pizzeria onto Uri's face. "What you doin' man? Why you actin' all sketchy? You gonna freak my lady creepin', around like this. C'mon inside. It's warm. Your New York ass should be freezin'. Meet my Queen."

Uri entered the pizzeria after he made eye contact with the giant Italian above him. It reminded him of what one of his fathers was supposed to look like, except that Uri had a bigger mustache.

The pizza parlor had a dilapidated dignity that Uri felt was quite stylish. His eyes traced large cracks from the floor across the ceiling as if he was inside of a giant whale examining the ribs of the creature that had consumed him. Below his feet black and white tiles guided him to the counter with local sports clippings from Rome celebrating consecutive victories over the cursed Lazio.

Clive gingerly crept forward towards his Queen Laquana and told her that this was his new friend that had put up a great fight against the Irish. She responded by asking Uri if he was a cop. Clive began to sweat and made a comment on the heat of the pizza and of Laquana. "He ain't no cop, he just a cracker buster like me. Should have seen him." He smiled; his speech had regained its strangely musical parlance. It was something she loved and would never admit.

"If he ain't a cop, why he got that mustache?" She backed up and crossed her arms and gazed at him with an incredulity that Uri found quite endearing. He was beginning to understand Clive's attraction as she possessed a style her European sisters lacked. Clive had rolled his sleeves up and Uri noticed a tattoo on his shoulder. It was a cross weaved from vibrant green ivy with purple lettering and Laquana's name stenciled across the top. Then thick lettering praising Christ in the middle and then *Per La Vendetta Della Mia Sorella* on the bottom. Uri recalled from the tongue of his first-ish father that the phrase was a pledge for vengeance.

The side of Uri's neck began to simmer with the heat from her glare. He smiled before returning a shielded look and bowing his head with respect.

"My name is Jiři Slävøvic turned Uri when I was born in New York. Jerome Ironside gave me my name. I have come for my American adventure, and the Irish tried bring death to Uri, but I lived and met Clive McDermott, the mad freestyler I saw under a swastika. Now I am here in the pizza store with my primary father on the sign. Meeting you is the next section of my America." He raised his eyes to meet hers and lifted his mustache to reveal a smile. The Queen examined him thoroughly before pouting her lips and brusquely saying, "You ain't a cop, but you could still be a Yankees fan, talking bout New York like it's some bomb shit. I don't know kid."

"C'mon," Clive's voice whined in serpentine streaks. "He's white chocolate—I promise." He had stopped pacing and sweating. Uri smiled at the Queen and she returned his grin with half of her face. She kept the other half tensed in hostility towards Clive.

"Yeah, he straight. You know how to behave and shit, so you ain't from NY. How'd you get set up with this lil honky here?" She nodded to Clive and then the grating chime of a bell pierced the air. A pizza was shoved over a counter from the back by unseen hands. Behind Uri and Clive, the door swung open again releasing more of the pizzeria scent into the night.

A smiling, uncoordinated man in a black shirt bearing a cartoon identical to the one on the pizzeria's awning marched to the counter and strummed the eight silver rings of his fingers against the counter. Clive rushed to greet him.

"What's up, Guido O'Shea? You no longer my second favorite whiteboy—now you number three." The Queen smiled at the man in a way that made Clive whimper with enraged jealousy. Clive had never learned his real name because she would not tell him. He was too shy to ask himself. The man was taller and skinnier than Clive with facial hair that always hinted at becoming a beard but never did. Laquana reached behind her and grabbed the pizza box without allowing her fingernails to touch it. "This here Uri from New York, but he ain't really." She ducked behind the counter to get a piece of paper and Guido O'Shea gazed at the tattoo etched on her spine. It was the Chinese symbol for strength. Guido O'Shea was one of the very few people that believed in Clive and Clive's musical talent. He seemed dumb enough to O'Shea that he had to be marketable. Also, the thought of Clive's visage on a shirt atop a thirteen-year-old fangirl's nascent tits was too amusing to him to deny that it could someday happen. This image alone would guarantee Clive's success in Guido's mind.

She rose above the counter. He ran his hand through his always-wet hair that had been curled and greased to unnoticeable perfection. "Doesn't look like a Yankee fan. Why don't you tell that skinny wop in the back to cut him some pepperoni *speciale*? I got to bounce. Pleasure to meet you, keep it real Clive." He raised his fist into the air in a way that Clive instinctively imitated.

"I don't know, might be a Yankees fan with that mustache and all. You ever been to Fenway?" She hypnotized Uri with her scowl until he responded confusedly.

"I was in Norway with my primary father." He looked to the cartoon Italian smiling down to him from the menu and reflected, ". . . once upon a time."

"Clive, only your skinny white ass find someone more whack than you. Nah, I'm playin', you straight. Wanna piece of pepperoni? Free from the big guy upstairs." She pointed to the Italian while getting Uri his slice of pizza. She handed him the neatly-cut, seamless slice. "Don't worry about Big Brother getting mad for stealin' his grub, he only kill Yankee fans."

"Yo, Laquana, I prayed to Allah last night and he say next life I comin' back a member of the Red Sox." Clive spoke and Uri smiled.

"Don't be prayin to come back down here a batboy. Plus, Allah don't let you come back. You supposed to be chillin' with him and all your virgins. Course, if you gotta pray to get some ass then I don't know what the hell I'm doin' wich you any damn way. I give Guido a hallah while you unwrappin Burkas and prayin' to Pedro's pitching ass like yo skinny ass could eat im." Clive smiled and Uri tilted his head.

"Don't talk dirty to me in front of Mr. Uri New York here, it ain't nice to tease."

Clive coquettishly grabbed her wrists across the black counter, and she responded by torquing his arm until he was in overt pain while still flashing his smile. His clumsy smile that Laquana had learned to love. So cool because he gave it only when she was causing him pain. It was when she first noticed this that she realized she had loved him all along and got the tattoo etched atop her spine to honor him.

"Don't worry Quany, we gonna be straight in a minute here, I got a good feeling about Hahvad this year."

"Yeah, right, look at you, they have screenings for people like you. Motherfucker, if you was in front of a judge there's no way you even getting parole. Hell, I'd send your skinny white ass away. What makes you think you getting' into Hahvad." Laquana smiled. "It's been years since you was young."

For the entire life of Clive, he had dreamed of Harvard. Not the experience of attending Harvard but the person he would be when his time at Harvard expired. He would then wear a petticoat and luminous black shoes while walking the streets of Boston with an orthodontically enhanced smile, knowing that everyone could feel his illustrious Harvard past.

He had not been received into Harvard before he graduated from high school. It was an event that devastated Clive and his only solace was his rap career. He had a vision though, it was the glint that distracted Laquana from Guido. That thing that dazzled her to adoration.

In his dreams atop the turntable below the Nazi flag and in his ten-year-old twin bed he imagined being a hero. The great man that would save a Provost of Harvard University from a certain demise. Not the President of Harvard, mind you, but better than a dean. He would be the original gangsta. The provost though, he must be everyone's best friend. It must be hard for him with everyone coming up to him like, "Yo Provo, remember me from back in the day? I got a genius kid that gots to go to Hahvad." Must be mad pressure, Clive thought. What if his life could be saved though? What if circumstances allowed heroism? What if I, Clive Duncan McDermott, could be that man of heroic circumstance? The man of the hour. Then the Provo would have to say yes, affirm my skinny white ass and let me roll with the best of the best. Then I'd be set for life. Then Quanny would be dating a Hahvad man, she the only one find that funnier than me, no doubt.

Drunk, happy, and vicious customers entered the pizzeria and gingerly balanced on the black counter while focusing through the greasy haze. Outside, the sporadic background noise of St. Patrick's Day came fleeing in from the heavy night. Screams of sybaritic rapture mutedly bounced from the tiles on the floor into Uri's ears. Leeringly, he gazed at the current pack of Caucasians that entered the pizzeria. They may as well have been the group from the morning. Their tender faces shone of hair, defying the sun to give them an attractive tan, vibrant red lips containing crooked teeth doffed by greasy straight hair shimmering under black wool hats. They stood in unison as a chirping gaggle.

These white people were a strange breed. So violent and alone while together. They were the mirror of an American dream Uri had yet to learn to see.

They stood: Irish and drunk. None of them had been to college yet in their young lives and they had already made more than any of Uri's fathers had accrued during their lives.

The unacknowledged rulers of the world. Those who own the stocks that make the human world spin atop the finger of commerce. These Caucasian Americans that trounce around their city with the privilege not only of race and culture. The envy of a diseased and infested planet. He watched them as vague reflections across the shadowed wall of the Old World, celebrating their own cultural artifices with imported beer and cartoon Italians. In the sweep of this thought Uri discovered a new emotion to accompany his new name. A flame of disgust licked him like a giant alien tongue into a paralytic rage.

One of the whites looked over to him. Before now, hatred had been an abstraction he felt when reading books about the holocaust. Things of moral clarity he could despise with a complete certainty of the soul.

Uri began trying to charm Laquana with the pastiche of perfect Spanish he had learned once upon a time.

"I'm not Rican you know?" Laquana smiled in a way that made Uri understand why Clive fell in love with her. Uncomfortable, the Caucasians looked at Uri before rolling their eyes at each other over to a table where they ate in concentrated silence. Chomping the slices like starved alley rats smacking down over layers of cheese, grease, and meat.

Uri stared at them, so fascinated that he did not blink. One of the Caucasians looked back without ceasing from his sloppy mastication. If this were another place and another time, he would have said something, he would have been clever like in the movies filmed in Los Angeles and said in his most Bostonian way, "You got a problem tough guy." He would have said that. Then Uri would have backed away. However, there was something about Uri that prevented this. They continued to gorge on the nadir of St. Patrick's Day; too drunk to sleep and too tired to stand.

Laquana yawned and said, "Where you stayin tonight New York? Clive's Mom ain't dead, is she?"

"I do not know. I had American friend in the morning, but he sent me for adventure."

"Clive'll hook you up. He seems to like you." She winked at him.

"Actually Quanny, I was wonderin if maybe Uri spend the night over the store. I wanted to spend some time with you. Too late to go home. All the micks are out driving." Clive blushed and rubbed his tattoo, it was his nervous habit and source of strength. When he got into Harvard, he would learn how to stop that, too.

Laquana lifted her lips over her shimmering teeth in ecstatic irritation. Above the head of the cartoon Italian there was a small room and a sink from when the pizza place had been a dilapidated nursing home. The owner had been an honest and evil man delivering only the explicit services he said he would to his clients. Born to bottle-a-day functional alcoholics in the Midwest. Fortunes blew his way despite himself. One day he found he had arrived in Boston after his second divorce with no children and a piece of real estate too large to comfortably live in alone.

The nursing home residents ate enough, watched television loud enough so that they did not have to talk to each other, and slept long nights besides vaguely illuminated pictures. The home was kept almost entirely dark until eleven in the morning on weekdays and ten in the morning on Sunday. This was to encourage them to sleep so that they could be fed the two meals a day they were contractually due. Throughout the night the overwhelming desire to piss and have a loved one back disrupted everyone's sleep, but this, like most cruelty, became tolerable with time and the residents learned to adjust.

The families would only come on Sundays after church. They walked by their mothers and fathers and gently whisked their fingers across their shoulders as if they were paying begrudging, doleful last respects to a distant cousin or business associate. After the viewing, that's what the owner called it, the men in the disparate families would convene at a bar tackily bedecked in Irish paraphernalia to drink and discuss the drudgery of life above the cubicles. Office managers to the core, they supervised by strolling and felt proud when stock prices rose. The owner loved Sundays because he would bounce three fingers off his gray mustache and smooth dark ivy brows knowing that he had made a strange thing stronger than heritage by bringing these Bostonians together. Eventually, the owner died earlier than his clients or he had wanted. His only regrets being that he never had children and that he would have been a smoker if he knew that this is all there was to life.

New owners came and within five years the neighborhood changed. The wealth stayed the same, but the faces were different. The pizza parlor arrived and swept away the stench of the elderly who had been forgotten before their pensions were fully drained.

Above it all there was a solitary room remaining with all pipes and wires intact and functioning. It was the place where Laquana and Clive had first made love after he had come in every day for two years to get his pepperoni pizza. It was not his favorite kind, but it was the one Laquana automatically served to him because he was her first regular and he did not want her to think differently of him.

After all the customers left the trio stood alone in the hazy psychological state when a long workday is about to end. All that was left to do was concentrate while that dull ache from the feet streams upwards atop the legs to pound on the skull like muffled drops in a bucket in a leaky home long after the storm has passed. The pizza parlor air grew thicker along with Laquana's longing to leave. She had never felt comfortable on St. Patrick's Day. Why, on this lone day in a culture both dead and modern, would an entire nation drink beer after dying it like slime? She had read in a Protestant pamphlet left in the pizzeria that the Irish did not invent St. Patrick's Day as the festive alcoholic shelter it had become, Americans did. The Irish just adopted it as another opportunity to waste themselves away upon the shores of alcohol abuse. That chronic thing that made starving families of six something other than an excess of Catholicism.

She sighed and looked at the busy hands of the dishwashers behind the counter. Her head ached with enervation and lust. That pull had always existed in her. Laquana's sister said it was the reason she had a whiteboy. Through the silver bordered window, the brown hands prayed and tangled themselves in a dish towel, like they were on the stage of a puppet show. Laquana looked at them and wanted to leave early. Wanted to leave now. She wondered to herself if those hands were something she could trust, if those hands were connected to a face of compassion that would let her leave before more people wandered this way. Turning her body into the silver window she spoke to the hands in broken Spanish, pleading and demanding that the dishwasher and cooker let her leave. He responded with a haggard "Si" more fatigued than she would let herself understand.

"Clive baby, show Uri upstairs while I finish up here."

"Aight." Clive winked at Uri and led him to a nondescript white door without a lock or a knob. Curling his fingers like an arthritic mendicant he scraped the paint away until he found the slit and opened the weight of the door by his fingernails. He sucked on his aching nails while enviously pondering the painted daggers Laquana wore on the tips of her fingers. They frightened him and he wished she would get rid of them.

On the other side of terror was a fantasy. When they made love, he would sometimes imagine her reaching down from her position on top to adjust him inside of her until she felt good. Then with a twist of her wrist and a smile cut his dick off with those fingernails so it would stay long and hard in her forever.

To dodge the thought of her he gnashed his nails against his teeth to cause more pain. The only thing that could remove the fantasy of Laquana at her greatest moment and inevitable betrayal. Biting harder on his nails, he felt parts of his ring finger slowly tear. Clive showed Uri to his new room and then Laquana took Clive home to her house where they would spend the next day entirely within each other. Ecstasy.

From the street, Giovanne's was illuminated with a dusty light perpetually kept on for security. The low glow infused every crevice of tile with a sickly hygienic luster that connoted stale sterilization— hard to penetrate and bereft of prosperity. When vagrants crossed in front and coughed out of instinct, the tone of light made them smell the hospitals they had all been in before.

From his lofty room, Uri gazed through a hole beneath Giovanne's mustache. He looked into the quiet black and white tile and tried to think of something and that something did not come. He tried to think of his homeland and skipped from black tile to white tile. He tried and failed to miss home. He missed his family—that is, he missed his mother. That thing that does so much more than merely create, the one that shapes without willing, that shames with a shallow breath and raised brows. She had been that thing that made him a man and she was not in the squares. He looked to the white square and wondered if his mother had even known he was gone. When he saw her last, she was senile and bereft of fault for anything.

Now things were different. Now he was like her, a wanderer in the misty limbo of desire and temperament. His eyes moved to the black square and he thought of her as a person. A base and cruel person. A person who became drunk and fucked men. Someone that does all those human things that people do instead of doing only those things that mothers ought to do. A simple human that connected, bonded, got bored and betrayed while moving between the shells of people in her life. Switching their faces like Russian dolls. Back and forth and then once more as if the pale dawn on the face of a new lover offered anything she had not felt before. Maybe she was the type of person that experienced the new in order to not remember. To replace the sand of memory with a new face so that she could forget what she was already standing upon.

It was all too late now because her memories had slipped to oblivion like sand through a child's hand. It had not even been erased. It had faded from recollection and from view of the mind and so from existence. All those things lost in nature's monolithic course of things. Those travels left relished and unrecorded in cerebral recesses of bituminous luster. They stopped being summoned to consciousness and were buried in the deep grey of a decaying mind.

Behind the steel counter emerged the Puerto Rican who took orders from Laquana all day without ever seeing her. It was easier that way. He did not want anyone to know. The boss had offered him a closet in the back that was always locked during the day so he would have a place to sleep while he figured out a way to get his papers or a wife. It had been three years since he left Puerto Rico with a flame he knew could not be extinguished and a tattoo across his chest of an unfurled Puerto Rican flag with writing beneath in beautiful Spanish that translated to:

Puerto Rico, so close to America so far away from God

The tattoo had gotten him assaulted by his countrymen, what-ever country it was. All of them drunk, speaking about heritage like it was something sacred in their blood. It was fine though, fun in a way, it was how he felt, it was a perversion of the cultural recol-lections of all those millions that came to America and could not be the luminous individuals they prayed to be. That island where he had grown up and become a man had only brought him to this point. His bed where he worked in a pizza parlor in Boston on St. Patrick's Day was the only thing holier to him than the church. He was in a terrible place, and it was a better hole than anything he had drowned in before.

There was something about poverty on an island that he could not stand. He felt disjointed and that at some moment between the wave's sliding on shore and the sun's tireless drumming he had missed some-thing. His sickly mother who had been saying she was about to die for twenty years was about to actually do so and then he really would have nothing. There would be nothing in his life but the sun and sea and beach against him without a family. So he left. He came to America and invented a culture of one. Melting pots destroy everything that goes into them. He did not have any money nor an identity that the American government could tax. He simply knew that he needed to be resurrected as a man and as an American. He would be born again a wealthy man who would create a son who would go to college. It was his life that waited just beyond the hope of his imagination.

He stood thinking about what it would be like to have a kid, a family, a Puerto Rican wife who could cook like his mother, and a son that would make him glow with pride. He thought of it all and smiled and then he thought of the price of diapers and how they were things he could not afford.

Uri quietly ventured out of his room and stared intensely at the wavy hair on the man from Puerto Rico who stroked it with gangly arms and quivering fingers. He felt Uri's eyes on him, felt it methodically drilling into his skull. He refused to look.

The man stared at the street and the specters stumbling home to sleep or to other's homes for sex. He looked at their long shadows through the pale hue of the light cast over the street like a forgotten spell. Squinting until late into the night when the smiling crest of the moon blended with the blur of the streetlamp and evaporated from the world.

Twelve streetlamps away Clive and Laquana were lying exposed to each other with their hands intertwined. They each marveled at the way the moonlight made her skin shine and his fade into the light. Laquana felt no individuation between her emotions and the gentle man she held and controlled in her grasp. It was also the moment when Clive had to repress the desire to push the woman he prayed he had not impregnated away, to feel alone in his own skin again and pretend that she was not even there.

He looked at her hand, marveling at the raw beauty reflected by the dew drops of sweat percolating above his eyes.

"You know what Quanny?"

"What's up baby?" He loved her voice, it was a container for him to pour himself into and know that he would be safe, always.

"I wish I was born black."

Laquana smiled, thinking of humorous ways through her own irritation. "I know you do Clive," she said, sighing to relax herself and him, "but you weren't. Yo ass is too skinny and that's why you thinks you know what it be to have discrimination raining on you all day, but it don't."

"That ain't why Quanny." He thrust his gawky arm across her thick shoulder, futilely attempting to pull her over to face him, but she did not budge. "It's so I could be closer to you, so that the last little shadow space of black and white would disappear and we could lie here knowin' that the world is against us for all the same reasons."

Her eyes winced with euphoria, and she arched her back and turned to him melting and flowing under the profound weight of his skinny white arms that flashed his tattoo of culture and desire to the moonlight. She kissed him, consuming his lips and made a promise to herself that she would never tell him he had a little white dick.

She would try to understand the Nazi flag he so prominently displayed in his room above his turn tables because it really did make sense in a Clive kind of way. She would do all these things and never again tell him while he made love to her that he would never fuck like a brother. She would do all these things, fulfill every promise as she mounted on top of him and buried her blue nails beneath his pellucid moonlight flesh that quivered as his muscle struggled to make her move to fuck. She cut him, watching her fingernails penetrate his flesh and glide in and out as he did to her with all his might. There she remained, floating in a moment of passion without ascension or regret. It was a pure feeling and more than she had ever felt before and it still felt false. She maintained it as long as she could before she hollered down to Clive below that he would never be able to fuck her, that his white dick wasn't nuthin', that he would never fuck her like a brothah. She said this and more, shutting her eyes until she felt the full force of her rage and lust swell up through her and out her mouth in a grimace of bliss and fury. Clive leaned his head back and smiled long enough to glimpse the dark sentiment of the ocean within him rushing to the surface in a cold current of wrath that breached the surface and wisped into the air before clinging to its place above and returning to the place below that had wrought it against the light for Clive's moment of redemption.

Laquana simmered down next to him and relished the sensation of warmth and power as his twig arm rested meekly around her shoulder. She was beautiful and black and knew all these things. Imagining what the moon must think as it looked down upon her with this absurd man whom did not belong with her lust for life, passion, and strength. She cherished the judgment of the moon, that wan white face so sick and close to death. She was the world that ghost above orbited around. Casting its light on her only made it more enraged and she loved that. Fucking in front of a sterile white face with her back to the Sun.

Verse 8

Clive awoke with the early sun glaring at him from atop the crescent shadow of Laquana's skull. His eyes fluttered and his pupils contracted into bituminous points that he buried into her shoulder that was stronger than his. Exhaling a palpable drag of the misty air their faces had been exchanging all night, he inhaled a euphoria over the destined future he knew lay waiting for them. A unification of the divine fusion that constitutes genius when imagination and will marry in sublime glory.

He drew another breath from the deep well of Laquana's mouth and felt the power to fulfill the American destiny that he knew was both sacred and owed to him. Since his first pubic hair sprouted in the nacre between his bellybutton and genitals, Harvard had shaped his life under a viscous shadow. He looked to the ceiling and thanked Allah, God, and Yahveh and beseeched them for the strength to finish this grand objective.

Placing a meek and gentle kiss on Laquana's forehead, he slipped from her bed as she smiled. He left the house through the window so he would not have to deal with her roommates who hated him for reasons he completely understood. Leaving through the window was best for Quany. When his head scraped against the paint of the sill he wondered if Laquana knew of the tireless sacrifices he had always made to her while she was asleep. If she knew of the innumerable hours that accumulated into days when he would watch her sleep into the post-dawn light, ready to protect her.

He imagined dying in her arms after a long and incredible life. All of it was part of the grand plan in his mind that would commence with Uri's great moment and conclude after Clive's ashes had been collected from his burned corpse and spread over Boston Harbor to join the dusty gray luminaries of so many before who had all helped create this nation from nothing. It was just as Clive would create his own life from a barren seed in a pot of clay. He would grow to be a stalwart thing, lush and green and strong so the rest of the world could rest its weary problems upon him.

He paused to glance back into Laquana's room, she had kept her childhood posters of rap artists and even had Michael and Janet Jackson when their faces could be distinguished. Clive wondered if anything had ever really changed in the world. If growing up, falling in love, that mammoth task of maintaining love, his mother, friends he used to know…any of it, mattered before now. The posters on Laquana's wall had not changed and neither had she. Now the future loomed odious and tall and she needed someone who had the strength to protect her and to sacrifice everything for a triumph of his will.

A rhythmic knocking roused a nearly naked Uri from his concentration and desire to consume a full pizza. Uri gently and happily swayed to its rhythm.

Behind Uri and within the dirty white wall a cat meowed, and Uri thought it must have been attuned to the same scents as he. They were the same creature, Uri and the cat, in that moment they shared together. Between the walls the cat was smelling and hunting a pregnant rat. Their realms, Uri and the cat, were both in purblind darkness where only the shape of things could be detected and never the actual form. Uri imagined the wonder of existing in that realm where sight no longer mattered. What if scent drove us forward, compelled eroticism, determined where and when we ate, where our infidel spouses had been? He visualized the smell of a dead relative; his insides still being devoured by billions of bacteria despite the best efforts of the undertaker to maintain the physical simulacrum of life. Imagine what a corpse, recently deceased and not yet full of maggots always feasting, must smell like to a scavenger dog, starving and on the brink of rabid madness? It must be sublime. Uri wondered why divinity must be a piercing light that overcomes the soul? Why not have a smell indicate who is writhing in wheat fields of brimstone and who is dutifully marching into heaven? Hell was too tactile and heaven too cerebral. Uri was not certain whether the thought of Heaven or the living sensation of Hell, palatable to his nose, was a better alternative when he reached that point in the road of life when there are no more roads.

The rapping at the door emerged again through Uri's cloud of thought, softer and more frenetic, but the same beat that Uri could not prevent his fingers from tapping out.

Through the stale air he sucked in a begrudging sigh acknowledging that he had to awaken and create another unfurled day of adventure. It was in those few paces from the bed to the door that his spirit waned and he called in German and Czech and Russian and Italian for all those European places he had dwelled without prospering but had managed to live and live well. He mused that in America one could choose to be poor, but if the choice was to be rich, it was a hard choice indeed and beyond one's obvious control.

As the door opened, the room filled with vibrant air, redolent and crisp, devoid of the greasy pizzeria haze that still clung to Uri's skin as if it was a series of barnacles drowning in the air.

"What up, killa? You sleep aight?"

"I like to enjoy the sleep, thank you."

"Coo, coo." Clive was sweating from a morning of pacing and deliberation. He looked at Uri with hope and pathetic pity. "C'mon, killa, I want to show you my main project. It is the song that makes the world go round, then go bounce."

"I am sorry, these are moments that I do not understand you." Uri gruffly ruffled his mustache with his hands and paused and noticed them. They seemed foreign to him, like they belonged to a far wiser man with a home and community.

"This thing, you see, this part." Uri stroked the back of his hand. "What is the name it has?"

"Nothing, man. Quit trippin'. It's the back of the hand, yo."

"Ah, yes. I see, well it is very funny, you know the American idiom, 'I know this like the back of my hand.'"

"Yeah, man. I know, I dig."

"Well, it is a lie, look." Uri grabbed Clive's hand and gingerly brought it just under his nose. The silhouette cast by the duo in this moment made Uri look like he was about to win the heart of the fair, ugly, virgin.

T'was the morning after St. Patrick's Day in Boston. Uri and Clive drove slowly amidst the low buildings of the city streets while feeling the cumulative hangover emanating from the brick and hollering from the mortar.

Quietly they stopped in front of Clive's childhood home. The place no longer shined for Uri, and it looked like so many dirty German homes built after their last grab for glory. Too new and filthy to be antique and lacking the innate reverence that vibrates from the moss-addled stones of buildings that know they have historic worth. This house of Clive's, house of his mother, could not be more than two generations old. It had slipped and lost the shimmering novelty of so much of this new and wonderful land. Now it was dilapidated in that distinctly American way.

Clive gingerly shut his car door and slowly crept forward as if he were a recently released convict. When he reached the front of his house, he unlocked the door and squeezed it hesitantly and then remembered the time when the Asian kids wired the doorknob to an electric current and then bet him he could not hold it. He had hated them for that and their mongrel eyes and unwavering studiousness. Then there were those test scores, always outstripping him. There was an innate brilliance that should accompany high test scores, that nonchalant dreamer in the back of the class who can waltz through the invisible boundaries that surrounded higher institutions of wealth and learning. Working for a test was wrong. The test should reward the innate.

It was all going to work out though, test scores and grades were nothing compared to a man's life. He had started to love the Asians as if they were his brothers because they would all be going to the same university soon.

Clive strolled noisily through a dirty white door and Uri stood back and was surprised to find Clive's mother with a cracked high ball glass through which an ounce of diluted scotch slowly bled along the blue veins in her acrid fingers. Across her face lipstick had been smeared as if she had spent all of St. Paddy's Day pretending to be a prostitute she had seen in a movie once.

Uri thought of his mother again, born to struggle, but with the gift of dignity, that thing royalty used to have until it saw the peasantry getting divorces and became envious of the freedom. Clive's mother definitely had it. The proof was smeared all over the woman's face in the wilting dark color that roses assume moments before a human hand decides to bury them in the trash.

Clive's heavy black boots made each stair creak in an off-kilter rhythm while the woman passed out in the chair snorted so that she would not choke. Uri looked over at her through the dusty banister and touched it and disturbed the gentle dust to reveal the shimmering oak that Clive had not felt since he was a boy. He meditated upon the house, the woman, the country, the friend, and felt grateful that he had been born as a pastiche of language and culture who was incapable of knowing the innate shame in any land.

Shame reeked from every pour of Clive McDermott's tallow flesh. There was something about the people of this city, they could smell it on Clive. Clive smelled it on himself. He knew that he stunk and that he lacked the cleansing properties of wealth, education, or lineage. Shame to be born into a world of infinite opportunity within a city of tiered barriers.

Uri's meditation was interrupted by Clive hissing and erratically gesticulating for Uri to move his eyes away from the woman in the chair and to join Clive in his room. Uri did not like moments of lucid tranquility to be disturbed, but what could he expect from someone of Clive's breeding? Lowering his head to accommodate a tired sigh, Uri imagined who he would meet next. He remembered once when his finger, shadowed in candlelight, chased its way west atop a map and against insurmountable geographic and human obstacles. Uri continued up the stairs noting the silence his footsteps made in comparison to those of his new American friend.

Uri was tired because Clive was tired, but as Clive would repeatedly tell him, "You get your rest only after the storm showed its shit."

Within Clive's room Uri was exposed to a cacophony of ideals and images that would have made Laquana blush but not with shame.

Uri was privy to it all because Clive needed him. After Clive explained everything, Uri reached the end of the narrative of him, his life. This man who bore a tattoo as his identity and now wanted a new one. Uri had never experienced being a father before. Yet, in the still shadows of this cramped and bristling groom was a chance to see a creature awake from the stillborn ashes of his crushed adolescence. To be born again was how Uri would later understand it.

While listening, Uri's eyes opened larger than the ambit of his imagination as Clive told him his everything plan to shape the face of America, to bring down the white man, to go to Harvard, to become someone, to launch his hip hop career. He told everything that had been percolating in his unspoken dreams, bursting with enthusiasm at the destiny he knew had brought Uri to him. His hands waved in fast, emphatic, jostling motions like a rabid squirrel looking to bite something before its own demise.

Uri looked for the swastika that always watched over Clive and was perplexed by its absence. Clive had removed it to reveal a large flatscreen television nestled comfortably into the wall.

"Yo, Uri. Yo Russian ass ain't gonna believe this."

"Russia is not even Europe." Uri grumbled in heavily accented English that he knew Clive would not understand. Uri's eyes gazed at Clive as he sought something redeeming for a splinter had emerged between the American experience for Uri and his personal sentiments for Clive. Now, Uri wanted to move to a new place, a new city. His ascending disgust compelled him to a new adventure. Uri looked

to Clive again while massaging his mustache that he had been considering dyeing a new color.

Clive turned on the screen with a remote control he hid under
his pillow next to a long machine pistol that helped him have sweet
dreams. He was less terrified of guns than he was of other people and began studying them around the time of puberty when he
first realized that he was physically weak. He didn't view guns in
the technical mode of a powerful weapon shredding weak animals.
Rather, he enjoyed the cinematic criminal that chose the exact gun
for his outfit. Chilling, silver-plated pistols made by old nephews of
gangsters in Italy went well with Panama suites tailored in Miami.
Smooth, black shotguns with the barrels expertly sawed-off accen-
tuated men, bronzed by the sun and life, with spotless white shirts
and cool, black European shades. One was morally required to lift
weights in order to own a magnificent gun like that.

The weapon was only as potent as the style of the man wielding
it. Thus, Clive was not a man for sawed-off black shotguns. Clive
knew that once you found your gun style all that was needed in life
was access to clean, sweet water. Boston, Appalachia, Africa . . .
gun style was more than the destiny of a man, it was the destiny of
a nation that defined the individual. It was the nation that gave life
to ambition and talent. Without the nation there would never have
been the first genius. Without the nation the work of the first genius
would never be remembered. The greatest tragedy of man was
that the name of the tribe that invented the proper noun had been
effaced from the memory of those that needed it. Such luminaries
were pushed aside for mathematical prodigies who gave the world
nuclear weapons and then nuclear power. Einstein is the jetsam that
floats on this wonderful American sea. His achievements and his
carnage should not inspire the heart of man, so Clive thought. The
man who birthed the tears of Hiroshima, the genius who ended
the status quo because he sat, bored and alone, in a Swiss patent

office, did not deserve our praise, that grand pacifist who never shot another human was the architect of so much more. Perhaps our greatest American failing is that posterity and progress are things that do not seek virtue yet leave its simulacrum in their wake.

Einstein would never have been able to carry a gun. He had no gun style. There was just not a gun for the style of the joyful genius with no comprehension of what he has done. It would be like God wearing a pistol while ripping Adam, alone and screaming, from Paradise and tossing him onto the dusty stone loins of the Earth below.

Clive smiled as he imagined what the world would be after he unveiled his triumph to Uri. He imagined a world made in the vision of Clive, a revolution fueled not by tyranny or guns, but by disgust.

Clive could literally taste his own sense of disgust. The sublime precursor to social change had been looping on his tongue for years. He savored the flavor of the potential for his suicide. He looked at America and saw the most powerful and prosperous nation that had ever existed, a being of such brilliance that there was not a soul in existence who opened its eyes for the first time and would not feel its influence tickling its spine. Then he looked inside himself and his nation and he felt a tremendous depression for it was a nation of legal drug addicts and moral junkies. Depressed people who could not continue to lie to themselves to spend one more day in a cubicle if it were not for those pills that ended the all-encompassing state of anxiety. Clive looked at America and wept. He felt the cries of others and he gave them an answer. That culture that had made all this, it had to end so that people could be happy, meaningful creatures as God had intended when he blinked for that one moment and Americans were born from the reflection of his eye. The nation of destiny that altered everything, this should have been the moment of triumph.

It was impossible for Clive, or anyone else, to experience what they should be experiencing. America was a culture that needed an enemy and its greatest triumphs were never done out of the ethereal spirit of creation, but from dogged determination to defeat an enemy even if the laws of science themselves had to be reborn. America had done all these things before. Just rinse, wash, and repeat…or so the story goes.

Nazis, communists, poverty, drugs, terror, the cultural memory ascended Clive's trembling esophagus. He raged. He thought of his veteran uncles in Southy, a cadre of awkward creatures struck with hacked limbs, limps and God's memories from a barbaric era that should never have been. The culture lacked the imagination to see the world as a place of creation instead of combat and the world could not restrain itself from those very natural impulses of brutality that insects deemed average and typical. Clive begged for his imagination to spread and breed. Thus, sweeping across vast planes of verdure, escaping all that was evil, irrevocable, and important in these modern days. By the year 2100 where would we be? The future no longer emitted the insinuated echo of a better time to come but gave to a salacious screech for blood. Time itself needed the death of boys before cancer could take them on. It needed to prove that God's greatest creation could never stop what it was. So, Clive felt the waves of future children hacked by machetes and precisely incinerated by bombs. Their innocence may end at puberty, just like his. Clive felt all these things and wanted to vomit. He flicked on the screen and showed Uri the culmination of everything that had been before. The world would be changed through music, like the Beatles. John Lennon could die a thousand deaths and it would never take away what he had given to all of us. So, Clive felt deep in himself and played his music video for the first time to a former stranger.

EXTERIOR SHOT: A black and white panning shot of post-carnage scene in Montgomery Alabama. White policemen walk about the wounded and dying black men like automatous ghouls. Static on screen then a pan going the other way of the race riots in Detroit (more carnage, fewer people, the flames obscure the racial features of the slow-moving people).

Enter the music, a lone reed instrument setting the tone of angst and change.

CUT TO: an unblinking eye in black and white, the new vision of America

Clive

Yo, yo, yo. It's just another race war, go out and rape a white whore.

EXTERIOR SHOT: Color this time, a debutant ball in the Pacific Northwest with patrician honkeys and their dates fresh from courses on manners. Their parents swarm around them, it is quite a spectacle.

Clive

Two millennia since Jesus dead, this is what we get instead, 18-year-old white bread, introduced to the whole wide world or society instead.

The world slowly dies, dripping blood red.

No matter, nothing does, atop this lily white head.

CUT TO: A brown woman's fingers slightly bleeding over a virginal white dress. She knows exactly when to wipe the blood off her fingers. Fade to a shot of the hands of a small Chinese worker skillfully smashing a cell phone to extract components for recycling.

Clive

Ain't no responsibility for a few million more coloreds dead. Can't protest what's already been done.

Can't let the government take away my gun.

Between the outside world and me,
scared enough to drown myself in the ocean, sweet lost virginity.

ESTABLISHING SHOT: VETERANS' HOSPITAL IN UTAH. Slow pan right of Veterans panhandling in disheveled uniforms outside.

Clive

Never forget, yo, before we breed another victim, fore we give another lost soul political down syndrome, that we just in time for a war.

CUT TO: Michigan militia, Black Panthers, PLO, rebel Columbian drug runners, Mexican coyotes, Chinese executives (marching in line), smug Europeans.

Clive and gospel singers (sing chorus)

Just another race war, go out and rape a white whore.

Clive

Business as usual in the U.S. of A, the whole damn world smiling, gonna make us pay,

History was born to make ash heaps; the new global culture better look out not to burn its feet.

Time again for the next great war,

Just another race war, go out and rape a white whore.

ESTABLISHING SHOT: Black and white, ethereal dresses floating from the sky like big flakes of ash. The scene is dead at first but gives way to all the cultures of the world that made America with its manual labor, coolies, niggers, and spics frivolously dance atop the falling dresses from the sky. A chain of Hindus enters dancing around the periphery.

Clive

Time for the revolution, to let the seas of white culture reach their conclusion.

Time for Europe and America to die by their own collusion

No more colonies, no more pride.

Sweep the wayward culture out to sea, let the big show rise.

Time to make white on white violence a hate crime.

Just another race war.

CREDITS ROLL

Uri's eyes twitched in a trifecta of mirth, rage, and passion. They all seemed to sputter through his mind at once. Painfully scraping across the top of his skull as they sought a word to give them proper expression. The word did not come, it did not exist in any language he had known until now.

Uri was terrified and curious, it reminded him of when his mother told him of her first sexual experience as a lesson against the libertine philosophy that had ensued after her nation's last great European catastrophe.

Clive turned the cool, blue screen of the television off and stroked his fingers over his gun. He noted the whiteness of his skin next to the weapon and glided over to his turntables and picked up his neatly ordered Nazi flag and folded it like he had learned how to in Boy Scouts. He gingerly returned it to its place of reverence above the turntables. He felt strength when he skirted his fingers along each ninety-degree angle.

"Well, what do you think?" Clive asked while he turned from the flag.

"I don't know," he mumbled and looked at his thumbs, then to the unbearable intensity in Clive's eyes that tormented like a coming sun stroke before he blinked once and returned to his thumbs. "It was really, really something. It is a thing that I do not have words for expressing." He looked back to Clive, whose intensity had softened as he saw the unsettling effect on a foreigner. If it could infect others across cultural boundaries it could succeed.

Clive felt a new type of power of confidence in the back of his throat. He had moved this European cowboy with his creation. The power of hip-hop had been to glorify the impoverished. No more cultural flashes to incite teenagers to eat what corporate America fed them. Now it would do something else, destroy the bitch culture that had repressed it and maligned human life into its current franchise form. People fucked like they ordered hamburgers now. Women judged like a resume by the clothes she wore and the diction riding her speech. Race was a social card. People only wanted franchise relations. Whiteboys never fucked the blacks, not in Bean Town; too scared of failing to live up to the size of any black dick. No, it was best for everyone to fuck their own class. It kept things simple and healthy. That order, that vile order needed to die. Now. Clive smiled. He held emotional control over Uri. Something Uri may have noted and let pass. Time for phase two of the life of Uri, time to get this revolution of Clive in the cultural oven if he was gonna blow it up. Clive felt exonerated through Uri's emotional supplication. It was an exoneration from life, from Boston, from that haggard bitch downstairs that paid his bills before he could just so she could criticize him.

There was no vengeance like success and this moment was his ivory moment of triumph.

Outside the sun shined and illuminated his personal hearth below the Nazi flag. That immutable thing that had already fertilized the earth with its seed. Now, it was a mere matter of distributing his video through that vast land of pornography and good, free ideas that were too hard to find. He would give his gift with a mere keystroke in a moment and since the only thing that time forgets to destroy is quality it would remain online for years, spreading from conscience to conscience, until everyone saw the world in terms of a singular choice with an unflinching answer.

"Yo, Uri. Back in the communist days how did things function?"

"I am not communist, you weaver of empires."

"Yo, I know, I know. You euro-K.K.Kats be mad democratic now, but I'm sayin, you lived under some communist shit. Right?"

"Yes, you and your type do not know."

"I know, I know. But how did you live?"

"Poorly."

"What I'm trying to say is . . . if you had to get some shit done, what would you do?"

"Wait."

"I know, I know, but what if you just haaad to get some shit done, like yo' mamma needed an operation or sumthin' on time yo?"

"I used to be in Budapest. The people there said that Communism does not work because Russian watches do not work. Nothing is 'on time.'"

Clive stroked his hand over his head, swearing at the outside traffic. It was imperative that Uri understand for the benefit of man's future.

"Aight . . . let's say yo Mamma need an operation, and you the head of the ministry of the cultivation of patriotism of livin' in the now, or sumthin'"

"Yes."

"Could you get your mamma her goddamn operation then?"

"Yes."

"Why?" Clive cast a Cheshire's smile and bobbed his head to his own soundtrack constantly playing in his skull. He had proved his point to himself and won the day. Harvard was now a palpable drop on the horizon.

"Because family and power mix in communism, but you do not understand my history." Uri sat back in his seat violently miffed. Every night his dreams were a pastiche of language and torment, memories of politics that did not involve him, adroit migration before a storm could hit. His Europe was one of shifting identity for the sake of safety. He had a gift for language because it was a necessity—everything else he could fake. Culture could be imitated; the effects of education were most readily found in a person's speech. All of this could be duplicated except for these American creatures. Uri hated the Russians, but he felt an acute kinship with them when their entire civilization was impugned by a twenty-year old American attempting to freestyle his way from Boston to the American aristocracy.

"I know I know yo, we Americans have no history, man. A couple hundred years and change ain't nuthin' like Europe.

But don't get all pissy man, I ain't fuckin' with you, jus tryin to prove a point. Tryin' to show the similarities our two civilizations got. This lil Atlantic pond ain't nothing to separate our kind. America the same as you. You might have been told all that jazz about hard work and then it don't matter who you are, because in America it ain't who you be, but how much money you got. That's democracy, man. All men are created equal as long as they work their whole lives for it. America's great because it's the only place where just about any motherfucker can soar past the sun . . . but if your coin flip lands on the other side. There ain't no one to pick up your pieces. Humpty Dumpty fall down in this here country, fucking end up shattered and washed to sea, no one ask about Humpty Dumpty again. You know, man? That's the deal here."

"I thank you for the information." Uri chirped, delighted. Clive glanced over at him while flipping his sunglasses open and putting them on his face, poking himself once in the eye.

"Now, you take a K.K.Kat like me. You seen my digs. I'm aight, but I was born into this American dream with nothing really, but the shit God gave me between my ears. You understand me, son? So, I see this big American dream, and I feel like I'm walking around a room where everybody just sleeping, having their dreams and nightmares, everything that America said it would give them. I'm walkin' through this room, Uri, and I want to sleep too, man, I want to sleep with these people. I look at my life, I look at all I've done, and unless I get into Harvard it's a flat line until my heart really dies. You feel me, Uri?"

"I believe I understand."

"That's good, man. That shit makes me mad happy." Clive smiled and nodded. "You think you could help me out playa?" He looked to Uri, his imploring brows raised above his glasses.

"Clive, I like you, you good friend, but I do not have many money."

Clive smiled and said, "What I need don't take money, just a favor for your friend America."

Verse 9

Clive drove Uri in his car and Harvard beckoned. Its aged stone flinted through the beer-tainted miasma of the St. Patty's Day aftermath and Clive drank it in. He would go and grant his surname retroactive prestige as if his great-grand-whatever were the first to hop off the boat from that Old World and onto this fresh new land. Social ascension was an intangible bliss that this European could not know. Perhaps that was why he sat here with his head bowed before Clive.

"Yo, Uri, cheer up dawg, we goin' to Hahvad today, then everything be nice." Clive smiled and slid his hands through the air as if he were performing in a theater.

"Harvard is good school. You went?"

Clive smiled unsymmetrically, less ashamed of his stained teeth. "The future, Ur, it's all in place in the future." He paused and reflected. "So, Uri, you know when we was jivin' about commie life and all that jazz?"

"Yes, I am recalling."

"What do you say bout helpin' out this funk soul brotha, climbin' them ivy walls of green?"

"You need Berlitz tape, really." Uri clenched his skull with the vice-like grip of his fingers.

"All I'm sayin' is, how would you like to help this here playa make his dream come true, make the dream of his family come true?

You're European, you know 'bout Aristocracy and the virtue of blue blood pumpin' and jumpin' in your veins. Help me do one thing and it'll all be nice, for real."

"I do not help you make crimes." Uri had squeezed his temples until Clive's meaning spurted into his psyche.

"Make crime, you a funny dude, Uri. You commit crimes. C-O-M-M-I-T, like marriage or sumthin'. Crime in America be a commitment. Ain't no chump thang, Uri."

"I am not getting a wife, and I do not C-O-M-M-I-T anything for you, I am sorry, new American friend."

Uri suddenly and desperately wanted to sleep.

"Aight playa, I understand. I want you to do some shit that ain't wholly on the level, it's true, yo. But how bout dis' how about we do something where no one gets hurt, nothing gets stolen, and everybody wins. Sound fun?"

"These things, I accept."

"That's what I'm talking 'bout." Clive's spastic enthusiasm ignited Uri's spirit. "Now, here is what we gotta do. I want you to behave like a scary motherfucker. Can you do that, can you act like a scary motherfucker and not Baby Huey for a second?" Uri had acted once for very little money for a few Russian guards on the street. They were the type of young men who seemed to be born without youth or innocence. Uri glared at Clive. "Shit, man, no need to kill me, that's the shit I need though, that's the shit I feel in yo soul, my motha fuckin' man, my negro, praise be Allah and all that jazz. Now, here is what I want you to do. I need you to pretend to rob someone, an old man, an intellectual, weak and scared."

"No."

Clive paused. "Will you let me finish? Can I finish? I need you to pretend, P-R-E-T-E-N-D to rob an old man, and then I need you to let me kick your ass."

"You mean you want to be hero for old man."

"Sicuro, dawg, you the real deal."

"Your father?" Uri inquired, certain.

"Uh no, a Provost at Harvard."

"Who, what is that?"

"He the playa behind the scenes, the gorilla soulja that gets things done."

"So, I make him scared like a girl, crying every day, and you get to study in the Harvard."

"You got it, babe."

Uri nodded his head with incredulous approval. Anything so stupid and dastardly must be noted. "He is smart man, to be provosh of Harvard, no?"

"Uh, yeah, pretty up there in the clouds."

"I have experience with the provosh class, they do not have belief for coincidence."

"I got it under control man, no worries."

"You be the hero when you are little, people ask questions. Hero and power are brother and sister."

"That a Czech phrase?"

"I do not know, it is from the heart of Uri, the Czechs should pay me."

Clive clicked his fingers across the brown, plastic steering wheel. He had a plan, he knew it. He also knew it would dissipate like history if he mentioned the specifics.

Uri continued, "In addition, why should I become refugee in Boston, hiding from people, I went here two days, and I already am hiding."

"That's it man, you do this, this thing that ain't no crime, but ain't legal, you do this for me, and I'll give you my ride."

Uri thought of a horse, then modern times, then a car. "I can have car?"

"Yup, get comfy, but only if you get me the American dream, what do you say?"

"If I get car, I am half-American. No one will die, no money, just culture, a transaction of the culture?"

"Absolutely, and I'll send you down south, outta here so there be no Uri when the 5-0 comes creepin' up on you."

"You sure this man, the provosh of Harvard will not see everything like it is."

"Trust me, he won't know no thang."

When Clive and Uri arrived in Cambridge they were silently happy.

"Ok, twice a week, today be his lucky day, this K.K.K.at walks up from the Kennedy school of Government at 4:30 on his way home. I fantasize it's a tryst or something, and he be hittin' brilliant, hot semitic skinnnns, but it's more likely an end of the world cocktail party. All dem K.K.K.ats sit around like they be old school freemasons or sumthin'" Clive paused, rolled down the car window and hastily ignited a cigarette.

"So, aight, bout 4:45 he will walk there right under the streetlamp in front of us, see it, Ur? Right there? He will come strollin' like he ain't got a care in the world, and he don't cause he a Hahvad man, and right then, you jump him and scare him, I mean scare him bad, ask for his wallet, his soul, his life, whatever. Got it?"

"And?"

"Ok, coo, you got to scare him so bad that he cries for help. Make sure he means it, too. Make sure you shake him up down, sideways, wherever, so much that when this man cries for help he said via con dios to his dignity already. Capisci?"

"Capisco. And?"

"A man who gives up his dignity is a vulnerable fellah, do just 'bout anything to get it back, including hookin' my soulful ass up."

"Dignity is the thing I am born with, I understand, and?"

"Aight, aight, you a cool-cucumber-customer, y'know? Aight then I come and shake your shit down, and you resist, but not too much, and den, and I really hate to say this, you gonna have to let me punch you . . . don't worry man, I'll hit you gently on the side of the head, just gotta look real so dat he believes I saved his life. Then you run away around the corner and get in the car to drive the fuck outta town. I made a map for you last night."

"A man that believes in my destiny. This thing I like." Clive wet his lips and uncomfortably agreed with Uri's assessment of him.

"You understand the plan man?"

"Yes."

"You ever been to the South?"

"It is not possible."

"You ever been to Germany?"

"No, but I speak German."

"Close enough. Get ready to take a trip through history. God speed son, it's been real. The future be blinding like the sun."

Clive handed Uri a series of maps marked with one pink marker line that had been drawn continuously through them all.

"Yes! I am ready. I do, let us dance." Uri pushed the door open and was enthusiastic about stretching his legs. He wanted to gaze through the wan light of the streetlamp. Before Uri could do any of this Clive grabbed his arm.

"Yo, we got eleven minutes. I been saying our boy be like clock-work. Give him a little then you strike like a thief, like a Russian." Clive looked to Uri, wanting his approval.

"I am not . . ." Before he could finish his sentence he understood the joke and knew he was destined to make it to the South, whatever that meant.

"You Ur, you my dawg, you know?"

"I am thinking to understand you better in the next life."

"Nah, I mean, we be mad tight, right? Right man?"

"Yes," Uri said, unsure of himself.

"Here is a little present I got for you, help you with your English." Clive handed Uri a crinkly white bag containing a spiraling mass of country western CDs. "The crackers down south eat this shit up. They love it more than their debutants, whiskey, and college. Should help you on your way, put the a's and an's in the right place. Give you something to discuss around the ol' confederate campfire."

Uri looked at the CDs and their covers, clad with various country western singers striking sultry poses.

"They are girl cowboys, the hair, it is long and beautiful like a woman?" Uri scratched the surface of the CD, certain that the light from the street was altering things.

"Nah, they ain't girl cowboys, they're Texans, or something like dat, all dem honkeys down south listen to that shit. You speak like that, and you be nice Uri, oowee, I just know it."

Uri was touched and an emotion consumed him in a stalwart wave. He felt something impossible to fake or create even if he could have imagined how to do so. "I thank you, as do my fathers before now."

"I understand, yo, we be in touch. Just look for me on the five-O-clock razzle dazzle news tomorrow from Dixieland or wherever you be. But I knows you goin to Blacklanta first stop baby. Sherman's big black baby bitch bein all modern now, you in for a treat, this ain't no Eurostyle flavah. We be keeping real from here on to eternity, I be feelin you always, you my dawg, Ur."

The two men relaxed in the car seats to enjoy their last moment of stasis before life would change forever for both. Clive had lusted after this moment for years. A secret covenant of personal vengeance for being born outside of the aristocracy that crawled and schemed inside of the soul of every Harvard cadet. Uri pondered that this was just one more face card in the deck he had to pull to continue onwards to that wonderful thing he could not taste in any language but knew with the certainty of life itself was there.

Through the small crack in his window, Clive heard the distant whistling of his man from Harvard. He always did a different tune under the same melody. Clive wondered if that was part of the secret that was part of his genius.

"Aight, my man, you hear that, that the sound of nice times to come, share the bliss baby, that's how we be." Clive started the car and pulled it around the corner and paused to think of the red color of the bricks that flashed under the light. He carefully parked it facing the road to Uri's freedom.

"Aight, Uri, I'm gonna leave the keys in the ignition and go around back, he be under the light in less than a minute, God speed baby! God speed." Clive vanished into the evening. His sneakers gave no noise. It reminded Uri of an adroit goblin he had read about in a Czech fairy tale.

"It be showtime, huh, Clive?" Menacingly, Uri plucked a gray hair from his mustache while looking into the faint light of his reflection off of a scratched glass mirror. He had to become a criminal again, just for a moment, to channel the foreign personality of street violence so unnatural to his soul, but not his taught body; a skill forged by an exhausting life of need, adventure, and triumph. He looked to the shining keys gingerly wagging in the ignition, tempted, he looked back into the mirror to chastise himself with his eyes for allowing the side of man that roams uninhibited without honor into the moment. The whistling increased until it felt too loud. Uri exited the car mumbling prayers from different languages he had heard but not learned.

He had turned the corner when the car door finally clicked closed. Uri saw his quarry directly under the spotlight of the streetlamp. He was whistling without even an insinuation of joy on his face. It was a sight that deeply troubled Uri as he had learned that men who whistle without joy were not easily trifled with. Cautious and swiftly, Uri approached the whistling man.

"Hey motherfucker, give me your wallet, you motherfucker." Uri growled, allowing streams of drool to escape the corner of his mouth.

"Excuse me, St. Patrick's Day was yesterday. Be a good little lad now and remove yourself from my sight, then the sight of God if you have any dignity."

Uri increased the length of his spine to allow the whistling man to see his full height. He was half his size and twice his age. Uri was certain that he had misunderstood. Berlitz tapes needed to cover a larger range of topics.

"Move or be moved," the whistling man said, his voice now imbued with a grating frost that sounded of supernatural origin.

"You do not understand, I get your wallet now." The tide of emotion had swayed as this was no longer for Clive but an affront to Uri himself. Rage bubbled in his throat. He needed to go to the south, he needed to listen to country music, he needed to have his adventure, and this man needed to oblige by volunteering his wallet.

"Do you have any idea who you're accosting? I'm not like all things academic; they think I am, but I know better, and you should too."

"I do not have time for you, give me your wallet now." Behind them Clive slithered around the corner and felt the emotional tension on the windless street. He signaled an enthusiastic thumbs up to Uri to keep up the good performance. Uri acknowledged him with a squint of the eyes meant to bore through this Harvard provost's soul.

"Let me tell you something, I was in the great war, I broke nip codes and kept them from your Russian souls. The nips got me and I had to watch them extract information from my comrades in arms, and I had to watch the lil Japs squirm as they tortured me. They tortured me so much they thought that I knew nothing. They were wrong, I knew everything. My friends, comrades in arms, all died that day, and they all died after having implicated me. So, my big

Rusky friend, this is what it means to have strength. Not the vulgar ego you feel right now pumping through your veins. So please, fuck off. This is America, unless you have a gun pointed at my face, I wouldn't cross the street to piss out your burning corpse."

His granite voice riveted Uri. The Provost's eyes scanned the length of Uri's torso, freezing him in time and memory. He then started to whistle a tune that clenched Uri's chest. It was something from his past, a boisterous Slavic song sung by evil men after they did evil things.

The whistling man proceeded forward, ostensibly oblivious to Uri's unmoved, ferocious gaze. The man changed his new American life and Uri did not care for its bitter taste.

"I am not Russian."

Astonished, the whistling man stopped in his tracks and turned to look up at Uri, curious how he could still be there. The size discrepancy between the two men fighting for very different covenants now seemed comedic to Clive who swayed and snickered just out of their ambit. Clive thought that if he *was* an old short man, he would have given his wallet to Uri by now.

"I am not Russian." Uri repeated, less certain of himself.

"No, I suppose you are not. A Russian would have had the sincerity to at least try to kill me by now, but you are Slav, ja! Some degenerate Cold War hangover that even the Russians wouldn't want." He held a long umbrella that could only be called a classical umbrella with a silver tip that shined like a luxury bullet. He raised the tip until it was perpendicular to Uri's chest. Sensuously, he then ran it over Uri's shirt where it paused as if in meditation, blunt, small, and menacing. He started to whistle again and nonchalantly walked forward while flicking Uri's nostril with the tip of the umbrella.

A private insult between two men of honor. It was something Uri had experienced so often in Europe, unnecessary, done to merely prove a point that you are not like me. Our race and language may be the same, but you are something different, born into a caste you cannot name, but can smell every time I walk by your ilk and sneer. It was a type of thought Uri could not have imagined existing anywhere else but the places he already knew.

With an almost graceful flick Uri snatched the umbrella away from his nose and into his hand while using the full force of his shoulder to level his elbow into the skull of the whistling man.

Before Clive could think or react a Harvard Provost was at Uri's feet within full view of the wide streetlamp light. Uri looked at his peaked face, shimmering and drooling. The pink tongue, like that of a small dog, trembled out of the corner of his mouth, incontinent and fully exposed. With a fish monger's drudgery, Uri hooked the man's torso under his foot and flipped him on his back and extracted the wallet from the grasp of the stripped, fine Italian fabric.

Clive's body trembled with fear and tears. Something had not gone correctly so he reacted with panic, regretting not staying where he was as he rushed into the light to intervene in the one-act play he had created in his mind that was now beyond his control. The Provost dimly observed the staccato rhythm of timid feet approaching his face. He lunged his arm forward to protect his head and mumbled a curse that sounded like a prayer.

"What do you think you are doing, you scoundrel? Away from this place," Clive yelled in the most aristocratic manner he could muster. Uri looked at Clive. He stood, stalwart, as Clive cuffed him on the side of the face, the blow of an adolescent who would always be too timid to ever hurt anything. Uri stood, feeling betrayed by Clive. He had seen everything, heard everything. After all, this was his idea. Clive hunkered back, trembling and praying that Uri would leave.

Uri secured the thick wallet snuggly between his two fingers and removed a one-hundred-dollar bill and ate it in two bites. He then flicked the wallet into Clive's chest and nodded silently in a way that ensured Clive would never betray him out of a sense of fear rather than loyalty. He then briskly turned and walked around the corner and into the car and inserted the first country western CD and headed for the freeway south.

Under the streetlamp, Clive cradled the man's wallet and checked to see how much cash he carried. It was a lot. He briefly scanned the faces of Benjamin Franklin, too frightened to count the number. The Harvard Provost stumbled on his gelatin legs while grasping for a nonexistent handle on the brick wall beside him. Clive helped him to his feet and the Provost fell into his arms like an exhausted baby.

"Yo . . ." Clive paused. "Are you OK, sir? Sir?"

The man stood up and felt a sweeping tide of nausea once more before timidly responding and falling into the frail shoulder of Clive. "Thank you, thank you."

"I have your wallet, sir. I retrieved it for you from that thug."

The Provost took the wallet and scanned the tops of the hundred-dollar bills with his thumb, embarrassedly he closed it patting it securely into his back pocket.

"Did you, did you capture that thing that did this?" He was now panting, the sweat coming and going from atop his brow.

"No, but I got his license plate number. The cops will get him, justice will be served. This is America." Clive had written down Guido O'shea's license plate number in a neatly creased piece of paper.

"I see, son. Well, it appears that I am in your eternal debt. You seem to be reasonable. Are you a student at my beloved school?"

"No sir, just a regular Boston kid that never shined too brightly."

"That I can see. Here is my card. Call my secretary, we'll have a beer or something next week. Do you have a cell phone? Everyone in your generation seems to."

"Yes sir, I do." The strength of venom straightened his legs, his hand grasped for the umbrella that Uri had on his now plodding course south.

"Good. Call the authorities and have them meet me at my house. It's on this card, here. If you can get me that little bastard, I will be a happy man in my golden years. Until then." He briskly turned towards the direction he came, gently massaging the residual pain that flowed in vibrant pulses around his skull. He walked back into the oncoming night, covered by a curtain of dusk as he left the streetlamp. Not even his refined corporate shoes made a sound as he scurried back towards the safety of the place he had just been.

Later, when the police spotted Guido O'shea's car on the way to deliver a double pepperoni pizza in the vicinity of Cambridge, he was handcuffed and pressed firmly against the street, citing racism for the entire affair.

Then, at the police station, Laquana would be the only one who could speak to Guido's whereabouts, for she had been laying naked next to him. She spoke to the police about where he had been, and they asked her how she could know, and she told them. Clive would soon learn this and the glorious future he had seen so clearly, the one he could almost make, dissolved.

Chorus

A pitched wind taunted an exhilarated Uri outside of the window of the car as he descended south into the slow weight of heavier humidity. Voices across the radio's spectrum belched haranguing stories of Hell and evil and the gays. An epic battle being waged now and forever. Uri loved it all. He could understand some of the words that he had heard before, but the countenance of this new land confused him. The vowels were long and gripped like Velcro. Uri imagined the sweating man on the radio broadcast sitting behind a pulpit while he raised a damp handkerchief to stem the flow from his brow as the words poured out into the microphone in a steady and dulcet flow. Uri's tongue tripped over itself as his accent desperately tried to mold itself around the clay speech that emerged from the radio. He spoke slowly and without confidence until he started to wave his hand like an alcoholic conductor as the excited man on the AM radio must have been doing. In a flash, Uri imagined himself as Adolph Hitler standing on the podium and waving to the crowd. Every gesticulation calculated beforehand, a nation's looming rage and madness expressed in the singular downward thrust of the small man's hand.

Uri wondered why. To be on television would be nice, but to speak and persuade . . . that was the fantasy for him now. To express himself so passionately and eloquently that people would believe what he said, believe what he knew to be the truth. Uri sensed a palpable rift in culture and speech along his way down the map. He was possessed of a new mission and destination: Atlanta, Georgia. What had Clive said? "That it be where Sherman stopped to light a fire the South ain't never gonna forget, knowin' what you deserve and feelin' what you deserve toward different things."

The wind outside increased its struggle against the thick car window. Screeching slowly and then pulling back in defeat as the car slipped through its grasp.

Uri tore through the flesh of stale jerky and winced as it migrated beneath his teeth. When he was a Czech he heard a phrase after a meal, "the meat is stuffed into my teeth." Everyone laughed and it was true, beer flushed it away. On the long road to the South, he felt the jagged pieces of flesh that tasted like the smell of the gas station and commanded his tongue to make them move. They stayed and slowly dissolved between his teeth that began to shine whiter every day. Across the country the sun would soon sweep away its light for the night; then the same thing would happen in the next time zone and then the next and the next; until babies in Tokyo knew that it was time to sleep. Uri looked at his watch to note the exact instant when the setting sun mysteriously dipped below the sky and stopped warming his face. He looked at his reflection on the face of the watch again, faded silver that could never be coerced to shine, and looked back to the now-vanished sun. The sun would do this thing every day according to a designated moment on the silver dial of his watch. What was the exact power his watch held to dictate to the sun when it should die and when it should be resurrected? Uri had always believed it was the watch that followed the sun, but how could that be accurate when there was a human grid of time imposed upon all life as we knew it existed? How many hours in the day could the drive of man fill with toil and destruction? Wars used to be stopped by the changing of a season. Napoleon had to give his men a break when the winter came. It was the natural order of global domination. A sign of progress is that war could happen whenever now. We stopped the time of war through ingenuity. Did the watch combine with electricity to quell the night and tell the sun when it was time to die and time to wake? Perhaps limitations of man had met their final adversary. Lights went dark when they were told to, the sun set when mathematics said that it should. Time itself had become a property of socialization, why not a twelve-hour day by doubling the existing 60 minutes per second? The math still worked. Why did the world obey this grid, the fusion between how much light the sun had to give and the will of man?

If there was to be a rebellion in the future, the kind of rebellion that plastered sickles and hammers across red flags, the next revolution should be against time; against the fabric of life that says that if sex lasts an hour, it's incredible, a good movie should be no longer than two, and unless a person sleeps for eight out of twenty-four the work week of forty-five would be unhealthy.

Grumbling at the humiliation of having been subjected by the timepiece on his wrist, the same thing that subdued the sun, Uri turned on the radio to hear static that then sought a voice. It found it in the word of the Lord as the red car left the orbit of the Northeast and penetrated the cultural membrane of the Mason-Dixon line. The preacher on the radio wailed into a crescendo of perdition while his voice licked the top of Uri's skull from below.

Uri raced south in the central lane, blaring the country music CD on repeat until he memorized the song and could replay it in his head. His mother had been with an opera singer from Salzburg once who could do the same thing. He was so young that his baritone voice was honed atop polio-ravaged legs that would not support him. He sang operas constantly as his only expression of violence.

Uri blinked and noticed that the geography had changed. The headlights now picked out flickers of new vegetation. Clive's former car jumped with every pebble on the road and ascended over the next hill and into the dense trees in full bloom. A splinter of their glory cast like raining shadows through the scattered headlights of Uri's new car and into his mind.

Gradually, the repeated occurrence of the bold white words REST STOP stapled above reflective green squares lulled him to security and he took the offramp littered with gravel and large plastic cups to park snugly in between two monstrous trucks. It was his first stop since Boston. He looked side to side into the darkened truck cabins seeking someone to talk to and perhaps discuss country western music and this thing called the South. Then he turned off the engine, noted that he was perilously low on fuel, and slept.

Beside him in each cabin of the truck were two surly men, one white and one black, masturbating to the same erotic audio tape for truckers. Practicing their preferred way to cool down after a long day and night fueled by a full bottle of pep pills and distilled caffeine washed down by liters of Mountain Dew.

Back in Boston, Clive sat before his computer, exhausted. The Nazi flag was still there. He could not remove it until everything was final and typed out with official letterhead. Everything had been completed as correctly as he could make them and there was one thing left to do. Give his great rap gift to the world. With two keystrokes and a click he sent his music video hurtling into the only grand democracy for the world: the internet. The internet had proved to Clive that if you give people privacy and complete freedom, they will seek connections to their most base instincts.

Clive sent his work of art anonymously to the world. If it had no author, no grand architect that could be shown to be merely human, then everyone would feed off it, raging against the white with that feeling of disgust that a whole cadre of pharmaceuticals had sought to oppress with mind altering anti-depressants whose effects would never go away. There was a reason that an entire nation that knew no starvation was mired in depression. They all agreed with him. The culture of white had to be brought down. Evils one cannot taste are always the hardest to quell. But he would make his city and his nation taste all that was wrong with them. For the very first time, they would be born.

Song 2

A BOOM from the truck motor startled Uri awake with a sultry jolt. He instinctively started his car and then worried about gas. The spring trees were dense all around him with the thick sound of cicadas pressing the air and he briefly felt himself a part of this American thing, both protected and oppressing.

He inserted the next CD and continued down south while half-praying for gas. The songs were by a beautiful woman this time who sang about lost loves she always lamented never receiving while sitting on her sunset porch in Texas.

When he stopped for gas, it was the same sensation he had in New York when he stepped into a bold new world. Now he was in a world of t-shirts, baseball caps, and plaid.

Upon entering the gas station, he was startled by the sudden ring of the door. The shop was massive, vending souvenirs for children before cases upon cases of colored drinks that shined to Uri like royal gems. He feverishly examined the bric-a-brac until he stumbled into a rack of shirts on sale; their full price had been slashed by a thick, black marker. He needed a new style of dress to help him change from the place he had just been. Many of the people in the store had mustaches like his and this gave him comfort. He strummed his fingers over the shirts until he came to the large ones in the back, and they reminded him of the thick, black wallet he had held in his hands the night before. Its contents would have made him a different man in America. The difference between himself and everyone being a thumb's stroke over strips of paper. Then again, a few pieces of paper separated everyone from each other everywhere.

He pulled the shirt that would fit him tightly and handsomely. Across the chest in bold red letters, it read: VIRGINIA IS FOR LOVERS. He had heard in Europe that the Chinese thought that red was a very fortunate color. It was all the convincing that he needed. He went to the purchase line and snagged a cartoon map of America with different caricatures doing different things. A thick circle surrounded Virginia where two hefty hillbillies were making out on a hill. Next door in D.C. a large and serious guard kept a vigil over crying babies in oversized suites. He left the store whistling a melancholic tune that had been played in his car for hours before.

Back on the road Uri stared over the verdant, humid hills as a wide-eyed baby that can only react before it can speak; later placing words with the things that surround it and then learning to label the emotions it has felt all along. He noticed listless mammals that tentatively scuttled in the brush amidst leaves twisting in the wind revealing their green side that gave life and then the etiolated half that captured sun only when the wind turned it with too much violence. The slower he went the more he noticed dead wildlife on the road that were hit once and then again to bump them away. He saw this and sped up until he felt like a baby again and noticed a hitchhiker who was dirty and well-groomed and with too much luggage and a neatly cut cardboard sign stating:

GOING SOUTH TO MAMMY!

Uri signaled and pulled over to the side of the road and enjoyed the sound of soft gravel beneath the pausing tires. He listened to the man approaching and heard his large duffel bag drag across the earth. Uri smiled and noted that the bag was lighter than the one he had lugged across so many nations.

The hitchhiker stood at the window waiting for Uri to open the unlocked door. A ritual of the hitchhiker's code he had enacted a long time ago. Uri did not move so the man gingerly opened the door and asked Uri how he was doing and if he could bring his belongings. Uri said yes and the man stowed his bag and entered the car. Once back on the road, Uri turned off the music in order to hear everything that the man had to say. The silence lasted longer than he was comfortable with so he inserted a new CD. This one with a skinny man with an enormous belt buckle and a cowboy hat that shaded his eyes from the view of the photographer's lens. He sang in long, smooth melancholic verses that Uri enjoyed but did not want to hear now. The sound hit his ears like a sudden bright light after a dim dawn. The hitchhiker smiled and commented on the weather. He had the long beard of an unmarried intellectual and wore thick dirty clothes from the military a long time ago, yet the brass buttons still shined.

The hitchhiker had once worked as a petty thief during more innocent days. He knew his place, and he knew how rich those he exploited were. He never stole too much and selected his victims carefully for he knew that in the core of some rich man's souls was the consent and vision that wealth needed to be taken away because it had not been entirely earned through steady wages the way those nameless employees below paid for diapers and stale, awful beer. For his entire life he had traveled in highway skids up and down The South, making certain never to go to the same place twice. This was partially from a steadfast fear and mostly because he wanted every step he took to be in a new place with great novel experiences. A few times, when he had been drinking, he began to believe that we are all the same, just at different places doing the same things, confused at the universal frustrations of life. These sentiments passed with his drunkenness, and he was again ready to hit the road. Besides, now that even the autumn of his life had passed, and he still had never owned a watch, he knew that it was too late to see the world any differently than what he had known it to be since he was a child.

He lamented the way his nation had changed. Before, he could hitchhike easily and every day. A man could get up on the road with a sense of trust and the driver would be happy for the company. That was before the degenerate era of America. None of it was his fault. It was the hand of Zeitgeist that moved him now.

"So, where you from?" The hitchhiker was deliberate and closed in his speech.

"I am driving from Boston." The hitchhiker nodded.

"Never been that far North, always had the damnedest time understanding the accents of you fellas, the thing I figure is, the Mason Dixon wasn't just a line drawn by men, it was a jagged brush stroke from God. What you think 'bout that?"

"I do not know, what is the Mason Dixon?"

"Boy, it's the simplest thing." The hitchhiker looked over Uri's t-shirt to his doleful eyes. He looked at everything but him. He put his hand in his pocket and felt the dull edge of his short knife with the cork handle he had squeezed until it fit him better than the soul mate he never found. "It's the line that separates this land into the two things it is. The land of history and society and the realm of money. Never saw the need for the money part of the land, never saw why buildings would be made that don't make a thing but more money for more buildings."

Uri nodded in complete agreement.

"It seems to be the only distraction for ambitious men besides their wars. In a world that is not perfect I will take the buildings." The sweat from the hitchhiker's palm made the cork handle slip lightly in and out of his grasp. "You been to New York City?"

"Yes, that is where I began."

"Then you know what I'm talking 'bout, know exactly what I'm saying."

"It is a strange place; the buildings are a separate beauty from all this." Uri nodded his head to the hitchhiker to look out the window, which he did, noticing for the first time in years the shallow lazy streams and dense trees that had always guided him on his travels. Again, the hitchhiker looked at his shirt, trying to place him in the pantheon of human characters he had known through the intimacy of violence during his life.

"The South is different from all the others?" Uri asked, needing to understand where he was more than where he was going.

The hitchhiker vomited a chuckle. "Boy, those are true words, hell yeah, it's different, nothing the same here. Life here as different as a building is to a tree. You understand the difference? A tree grows, has roots, time can't stop it, the only thing that can is fire, that's what the North always knew, nope, never had much use for that type of thinking, that's why I'll stay down here, below the Mason Dixon." He paused again, the knife was now saturated, each porous hole in the handle had filled with a bubble of his sweat. "What's your name son? Never been able to take something from someone I didn't know, be it a ride or a life." He looked to Uri, gauging for effect. He detected none.

"My name is Uri; it is a pleasure to meet you. How are you doing?" Uri was not thinking about language now. He was channeling Berlitz tapes directly.

"Good to meet such a polite young northerner. My name is Billy Styron Junior." His fingers twitched over the knife handle with deliberation.

"I like that name, Styron, Sty-ron. It sounds like it is from the future."

The hitchhiker chuckled again. "Nothing from the future, just the past, bastard plum left my mom before I was old enough to tell him to go to hell myself, pardon my French."

"What did your father do?" Uri asked, thinking of the moment of his abandonment that he had recreated in his mind from the memories his mother gave him through her evening stories. It was a tremendous thing indeed to leave a child, particularly a father leaving a son, Uri had always wondered how men could leave the faces of themselves they had painted on another soul through fucking. It should be harder than leaving daughters, should be, but was not.

"He was some Northern artist type, writer or something, never saw the man's face myself. But he made me through and through. Everything I am today I am because of him, kind of strange, huh?" He relaxed his grip on the cork, stroking it compassionately with his thumb. "What did your pa do?"

"I do not know, there were only stories from my mother. They are not of one man though; they are several stories that have become one. Only I can tell the difference now because she is old." Hearing his words, the man released his handle on his knife and withdrew his hand, drying off all the sweat on the leg of his pants. With his other arm he grabbed one of Uri's hands from the wheel and vigorously shook it like a gentleman should upon an introduction. Most hands he felt were soft and unscarred. This palm was violent and different.

The car swished smoothly beneath an abandoned overpass with a cluster of gas stations and restaurants in an island overlooking the freeway.

"You see that up there? You see?" The man pointed behind the car at what they had just passed. Uri strained his neck to look at what his rearview mirror reflected with complete clarity. "Up there, right up there, I got this." Billy brushed away his beard to reveal a deep scar in his cheek. The edges rose up like lips of pink simmering lava shining at dawn. "A damn Cuban drug dealer cut my face and drove up on North in his BMW, cops didn't do nothing but blame me." The old man stroked the boundaries of his scar with his finger while Uri looked, astonished. "I always been on my own. But I used to be pretty and on my own like those fellas in Easy Rider. No worries and good looks, that's what life used to be about. Things are different now, I tell you." The hitchhiker relaxed back into his seat and sprung it back to give himself more leg room than he needed. He had received the scar more than a generation ago when he had seen a rich car fueling in the evening and the crickets and frogs were blaring and everything was so beautiful and still. He slithered into the back of the man's car through the open window and noticed that there were all the nice things and no air conditioning. Another Northerner thinking he was too good for what the Good Lord gave him. He waited and put his knife against the man's face when he had driven down the road and into the dark. He demanded his wallet, but the man did not speak English. He was carrying drugs to New York to fuel the vibrant Soho artist's scene before everything changed. The man did not understand anything and grabbed the knife and pulled out his own and cut crudely and without aim into the hitchhiker's cheek the way he had learned to do in Cuba to earn his way to America. Both men only felt the gash when the hitchhiker screamed. The Cuban left the hitchhiker by the side of the road.

In the glittering moments of that noisy evening that would never be still the Cuban regretted not killing the hitchhiker for his own safety. The hitchhiker stumbled back towards the light cradling his face and feeling the oozing substance of his youth splattered over his clothes. He knew he was marked. The scar of his physical weakness would be with him forever. He could not return to anyone he had known after that. His only recourse was to cover it with the wise growth of a beard shared by so many prophets. He did not want that, he wanted to live young forever until the moment he died. Everything he had done in his life had ensured his destiny until he had been given a new one by a man whose name he would never know.

The hitchhiker stroked his scar three times, a habit of reflection. He put his beard back into position and covered what he was from the drivers who accelerated past and the indifferent road signs connecting all points of interest that he dared to travel.

"So, stranger, now that we have that out of the way, tell me your story."

"My story?"

"Mmhmm, in my next life I am going to be a storyteller, so I need to get ready now."

"My story? You are writing my story."

"More my pa's trade, but a man's got a right to his privacy, only thing they can't take away from you. People say dignity is a thing like that, but dignity cannot stand alone, history and where a man puts his shoes at night make for dignity. Privacy though, that's just 'bout all we got left according to me."

"Maybe in the next life you will be a philosopher instead. It's better, no? In this country."

The hitchhiker looked to the trees and imagined the screeching birds he was missing by being in the car. He missed the country already. He nodded along to the rhythms in the car and the ebb of natural human life just beyond the boundary of the ruffling trees.

"You always listen to the same song?"

"I am trying to learn the ways of The South."

"Boy, this ain't the south—it *is*, but it ain't. The south is something else, it's something you can't feel but you can taste, you understand my meaning?"

"I do not think that I do."

"All right, this is great, real live fresh Northern meat and nothing but miles to go before we sleep."

Uri smiled, thinking of his Boston days that felt much further away than they actually were.

The hitchhiker turned down the music and faced Uri with his excitement constrained only by his seatbelt. "The South is . . . The South is . . . Where were you born, let's speak from metaphors, man can't understand his life or the good book without metaphor, where were you created?"

"I was born in poverty in France."

"Hell boy," he slapped Uri on his leg, "bet you were the original inventor of freedom fries. I always knew it'd be some story like that. Lost all your money from the corporations, too. If I had an idea like that, I'd go all the way to D.C. itself and knock on every door to make sure even the lawyers couldn't take my idea. It's the thought of a man that needs to be protected."

"I did not invent freedom or fries; I think they were both invented in my life though."

"Ok, ok, let's say you been born and brought up in France, you would think like a Frenchman, right? You look through the whole world through those skinny French eyes, but you look a little too big to be French by my reckoning."

"Thank you."

"Ok, ok, so let's say you were born in old Paree, and you feel the birth and death of an empire, you feel the pride and shame of Napoleon, you feel this in all the little things. Every time you fuck a little Frenchy in her short maid skirt you feel that history and romance, you feel chivalry and codes and right and wrong and art. We got the same things, just with a Southern twist. It's that Southern twist of life that makes it great."

"I was only born there, I did not grow there, I do not have these roots, but everything sounds very wonderful."

"You mean you got no culture? None to call your own?"

"I do not know; I have never thought of it in these ways."

"But every man got to have a culture, otherwise he got nothing to call his own. Where were you on September eleventh when those bastards in caves learned how to fly, lower than Icarus but higher than God."

Uri thought, "I was very drunk in Budapest, crossing a river over an elegant bridge during the night. It was very beautiful, and I felt like I was in a movie. Sometime I looked at all the television screens, they were the same."

"Boy, you do get around, I knew we was the same when I met you, do no harm to a righteous brother, I knew we were always walking the same desert when I met you. See, you got the same culture as me too, things felt different after that day, our cultures finally had a tragic chance to breathe together, that's what I mean. Now, The South is different, but you see my point, things tasted different after a moment in history, we all got our own moments to taste." Uri looked deeply into the road subtly being illuminated only by the lights of fellow travelers. The hitchhiker was correct, things tasted different after that day. Nothing affected him, and nothing was the same. He understood then that he was living in a world that he did not understand but that everything since that drunken night in Budapest had tasted differently.

"Thank you."

"You're sure welcome. The South is a different thing, but boy, it's a wonderful flavor."

A different kind of dark cut below the trees and Uri knew that it was time for him to sleep. He had been up for too long and was now feeling the timeless mood of the genius on the precipice of something spectacular. Uri's dreams were almost here. The all colorful and incoherent dance troupe that entertained him every night was soon to take the stage in his mind. Uri never had any use for night-mares, so he did not dream them.

"I am tired, could we sleep now?"

"Why hell yeah, we can sleep anywhere you want. We in The South, this whole land is my bed and this here forest is my blanket, protecting me from the infinite white eyes in the sky that watch us every night. Northern folks protect themselves with buildings, but what good is privacy if you can't stare back, watch them while they watchin' you." He smiled and gingerly opened his window to steal a peek at the nascent night sky before quickly moving his head back in. "Next gravel road you see, pull up on it."

Uri did as he was told and traveled gentle miles up an unpaved road, enjoying every second of the sound of squishing gravel beneath his tires.

"This spot here's as good as any, let's give this car here some rest. C'mon."

Uri followed the sound of the hitchhiker's banter into the woods until he silently stopped. Uri stretched his long arms out to look for a tree to balance on. He was suddenly dizzy and everything was black. There were no sounds and no light. He felt that all he had was the stomped vegetation trod beneath his feet.

Then he heard a few cracks as a small fire appeared from noth-ing and illuminated the clearing in a flickering orb of light. On the other side of the flame Billy smiled with a contorted contentment.

"In the West a man goes crazy, there's no protection from the eyes above. Folks out there is different."

Uri looked at the small gaps in the trees and saw only one dim star blinking back down.

The hitchhiker saw the same thing. "I'm lookin' at you too kid, but you can't see me, all you can see is my fire, and you can imag-ine it to be anything you want it to be." He handed Uri a decrepit blanket and a pillow. Both smelled of decaying food and had the sweet odor of a violent death.

Uri shuddered and remembered when he had slept while covered by much worse things before.

"Where you going anyway, son? Out West? Big frontiersman like you."

"I am going to Blacklanta."

"Hehehe, boy, you sure you weren't a son of The South God misdirected to ol Paree?"

"I do not think that is what God made me."

"Maybe not, but maybe, you never know in this world what makes sense and what don't."

The hitchhiker mumbled a prayer and took a swig out of his flask to help him sleep against the crackle of the fire. His flask contained exactly seven shots. They were measured out at the beginning of each week, and he shook the flask each time he finished a gulp to feel his burden lightening.

The shadows of the fire spread up the trunks of the surrounding trees. Uri watched the color and shape change when the flame lunged from one log to the next and so everything danced together in sole and sonorous rhythm. Billy blinked two lazy times and before the fire had finished casting a shadow across his face he had tumbled into his unconscious. Dreaming heroic dreams that were the delusions of politicians. Uri watched his beard change shape in the fire's light, how it squirmed and slithered until it blended with the soft vegetation he had felt through his shoes and knew he could sleep on it as soundly as if it were his mother's chest. Uri breathed everything that the world had to offer along with some smoke from the fire before he rolled on his back to stare at the lone star above and tell it in a soft foreign tongue that it need not worry about him. He would be just fine under its steady vigil that could never end but for the eruption of daylight all across The South.

Song 3

When Uri awoke the hitchhiker was gone. His belongings were neatly organized next to the fire that had uttered its last billow of steam an hour before. Uri blinked and looked for the star he had seen the last time he was conscious. It was replaced by a faded morning moon that hovered just above his patch of forest to wake him. He stood to sniff the humid air and stretched through the expected pain of sleeping outdoors. Curious, he looked back at the batch of moss and brush that had held him above the dirt throughout the night and studied it longer than he had his own shadow. He scanned the shape on the forest floor and marveled that this was his body. It seemed too large to be of this earth or to be of him. The morning moon glanced down over Uri's shoulder and Uri stepped aside to look back up and share a realization.

While nonchalantly strolling and wiping his eyes, he walked over to the hitchhiker's side of the fire to look for the imprint that he had made in the night and could find none. Again, he looked to the moon and received no response. Scuffing his feet in the grass he felt hunger and needed to decide whether this hitchhiker was a worthy companion for his American adventure. After all, what kind of American could live his life without ever owning a car?

The hitchhiker silently emerged from the forest and into the clearing using a silent path that only he could see. He was carrying two gray jugs that were cracked at the splintering neck saved only by a thick piece of dirty cork and tape to contain the contents.

"Got the sweetest water you ever tasted right here. Are you ready for adventure today?"

Uri picked up the hitchhiker's supplies from the campsite though he did not feel he should. The car sputtered and chewed through the gravel before landing on the cool hum of the freeway while the air in the vehicle became laced with country music. When the first song repeated itself Uri at last shed his concern over being deported for his Boston escapades. They would never actually have arrested him because he was not a terrorist, right? He remembered Clive and smiled and wished that he had a photograph of that silly little Caucasian dancing beneath a Nazi flag. Clive would be different now and memories can do nothing but fade. He needed photographs to remember things as they were and not as they needed to be.

Uri imagined rows of deranged students who studied every night of their adolescent lives to obtain Harvard. Then what? Would they creep into political office, or would they do the same things as everyone else here, only with the money and prestige of Harvard. An artist from Harvard and a bum on the beach could both coat squares of cardboard with beautiful, spray-painted scenes of the mountains. All the difference was in the artist knowing he had obtained Harvard and the bum wishing for artistic immortality. Harvard must have creative writing classes. Every subject there could not somehow be a seminar on how to take over the world. Could it?

He smiled and wondered if power and education were always the same things. If they were then history had always had very bad teachers.

"May I drink some of your sweet water, I am very thirsty."

"Sure thing, now you tell me if this isn't the sweetest water you ever tasted, sweeter than anything in the hills of old Paree." Uri uncorked the bottle and waited for a sound he had heard in

American cartoons. Disappointed, he drank anyway. It tasted of the hitchhiker's beard and fetid breath.

"There is no alcohol." Uri noted, trying to lick the taste off his lips so he could not smell it.

"No sir, you think I give a bottle of shine to a fresh-faced driver from ol' Paree? Life is hard enough without spitting in the face of statistics."

The day loomed brightly, an untold tale of new things and expressed curiosity, Uri rolled his window down to smell the difference in the air as it mixed with the airconditioned interior of the car. He took profound joy in rolling the window up and down and smelling the difference from the world of The South out there to his new airconditioned life in here. The country songs crooned, and the highways began to wind and turn on twisty bends towards the great heart of this thing he knew only as: The South. Small homes with large confederate flags flinted by. They drove over, past, and through forgotten battlefields where the roots of trees went deeper to escape the human blood that had once pooled above.

They drove through it all, oblivious, singing in crescendoed rejoice to the greatest hits album that spun again and again and recounted stories of love and ways of life on horses and prairies understood by all to be the artistic fabric that this whole great thing was cut from. A beautiful pattern that sewed itself onwards in a mystical procreation again and again before the sunset of the next generation.

"Y'know that more Americans died in the civil war than the war to end all wars, the war to liberate Europe from itself, the war against the Chinese in Korea, and that terrible war to conquer the minds of the Indochine?"

"I did not know that."

"Truer than any words a man can say are the statistics of a nation. And if you want to think about sacrifice, the war to unite this nation took more effort than any war to stop any evil. What does that tell you 'bout America?"

"It teaches history that war is a thing for young people to do when old people have not thought clearly about what they already know."

"That what you think?"

Uri thought back to his Berlitz training for an answer and found none. It was something that no word in any language could describe.

"Think again, cause that ain't it. The South knows its war and it feels its history, that's what makes it different. You'll see." The Hitchhiker reached to the dash of the car and shot the volume as loud as it was ever going to go to dance his bobbing head in the daylight. He rolled down the window and sang his own tune to the passing houses and thanked them for being after so much violent deliberation.

The daylight detail of twisting leaves began to give itself to the evening. The music was calmer now, the volume had decreased, and The Hitchhiker had fallen fast asleep. He muttered sweet nothings to a dreamtime nymph enthroned in his beard. She was the woman he spoke to when he knew he was truly alone. He was asleep now and in the darkness of his eyes he could not protect his shadowy spirit from Uri's confused grasp.

Coca-Cola and CNN signs emerged in a marching tandem down the road to light up the night. They were the stars people saw when they looked up now, fully lit so as to be as unavoidable as the North Star to ancient mariners. It was the global consumer fabric on which the fate of every screaming infant would rest its beleaguered head. All the European Bohemians that railed against the order of their parents. The streaming Arabic smoke in lounges with high-class pillows and insidious intent. The Chinese laborer who knew two English words: Coca and Cola that he would tell the wandering

American friend who dared venture to his village just north of Tibet. This was the lineage of The South.

Again, the signs marched side-by-side, telling the resident traveler that the realm of the highway was over and that a new urbanity had been reached catering to a greater thing than any one nation. Atlanta, the simmering capital of The South and the newsman and the beverage for an entire planet.

Uri now drove slower than he had before. He was compelled by a sense of discovery past his own trembling inhibitions towards wordless knowledge that the sparkling city lights were of a new and greater thing. Clive's directions had ended by now and so onwards he went. Straight ahead until the red from his gas tank's empty light flickered the same color as Coca-Cola's logo. The fuel in his car sputtered away as he pulled into an illuminated gas station. When the car halted the engine was silenced and the Hitchhiker awoke and said goodbye to his imaginary nymph who for years had been a more faithful companion than he felt he deserved.

The Hitchhiker was not grateful to see the world in front of his eyes. He knew without looking that they had arrived, and his eyes traced the road to see how long before he was back in the country and away from the sprawling heart of The South.

"Well, pilgrim, you've brought me to a place I already been, twice, and for that I don't know whether to thank you or not."

"It is always good to see the same place twice and say thanks because we do not really know how it is to be grateful until too much time has passed, these words are my mother's, not mine. And they sound better in the French."

The Hitchhiker and Uri stretched into the air and Uri licked the humidity to gleam his first understanding of what The Hitchhiker must have meant by a taste of The South.

"Never had much need for the city life, all the poverty with none of the freedom. I also don't care to walk the same place twice on the same path, I'll be leaving you now, lookin' for you in the papers." He handed Uri his flask and expressed his thanks in the New Orleans way. "Make sure you don't take more than one gulp, that's one-seventh of what the good Lord allows. I'm givin' you a good night's rest, and if you knew me more, you'd know that it's more a sacrifice than if my marrow were gold, and you sucked it to save your life."

"There is too much horror and beauty in you, good luck."

"Same to you, old Parisian. Same to you." Quickly capping his flask, he nodded to Uri and walked out of the gas station light to appear again as a shadow under the first Coca-Cola billboard he passed. Then he was gone. Uri filled his car with gas while searching for the sounds of the city.

Beside the gas station were two barbecue restaurants guarded by enormous trucks parked as if God had scraped his fingers through the asphalt and this was the result. Two kinds of music emerged muffled and discordant together in the night. Uri looked back one more time in search of The Hitchhiker while thinking that the two had an unfinished adventure to share. They would never meet again. The Hitchhiker would die in a way he could not have expected and while death enveloped him he would look back on his life and laugh. It was a silly and fitting way to leave The South, unnoticed and unburied.

Song 4

In the barbecue restaurant the unexpectedly lively neon lights beamed in purple and red. One sign, the one on the left, flickered spastically into the shape of an aggressive purple pig. The pig's companion in the other restaurant was a red dog that constantly shined day and night with its mouth agape in a constant act of aggression as if always ready to attack the pig. Both were protected by a rampart of scattered trucks that created a barrier like a chain link fence between two barking neighborhood dogs. Uri walked among the trucks and thought that they were better than a European labyrinth carved from overlapping hedges. He traced his hand along the different silver filigree of industry until the sweeping side of one of the trucks led him to the entrance of the barbecue restaurant with its pulsating purple neon light.

The glass door painted black by night swept three times after Uri entered to be greeted by a lounge of black truckers led in a rousing chorus by a blues musician. Uri thought he was listening to greatness and that in another life it could have worked out for that marvelous man. There was a niche he sat upon somewhere in the musical tradition spinning from the Renaissance Blues to The Jazz. He sang and played his sleepy guitar while telling the audience that in five-hundred years the lazy little kids will read about all us sinners in textbooks and note only that a man, a whiteboy, stepped on the moon and that God Himself delivered jazz unto us. Nothing else was worth a footnote because nothing else could last. All we were and all he could be was just a fingerprint on the soul of man, which is really a woman. After so many thousand years that you couldn't see how many fellas the great old lady soul had been with, but you still see The Jazz, the fingerprint right on the bitch's forehead.

The audience cheered as he strummed an ecstatic guitar riff with only the sweat of his brow and a few tightly controlled jerks of his knuckles. Uri nudged his way to the bar and ordered a whiskey in his most polite Berlitz English. The bartender looked at him and slid a beer down across the smoke-saturated wood.

"Three dollars. You want food?" The music swirled through the hovering puffs of cigarette smoke as the audience clapped together in one cosmic union. They were all truckers born across the land, united by their station in life and need to stop at the bar under the purple neon light anytime a delivery even smelled of Atlanta.

"I want a turkey sandwich, please?" The bartender scowled as if he had not understood. "I said I want a . . ."

"I heard you, boy. That's cracker shit, you want that, you go next door. We serve barbecue and only barbecue here."

Uri looked at the man and then to the blues player and paid for his beer. Curious, he stepped further into the haze of smoke and sound. All around him he noticed what could be the smatterings of Hell. The men's faces were covered with gelatinous, brown sauce that they licked off their upper lip long after it had been consumed. They wiped grizzled flesh towards flesh as they cleaned themselves between massive bites of a cow's ribcage, then a pig's. One patron picked up a fork and laughed and tossed it aside before draining the bones on his plate of the sauce that had pooled where marrow once was. Through it all the blues man played and beckoned Uri to go to the front of the stage when the demons with greasy fingers yelled at him to move out of the way in a fit of bloated rage. Uri did, he marveled at the traces of food that remained on the plates and were quickly removed by a cadre of waitresses who swam through the smoke and the legs of giants and returned with more barbecued flesh before the long night's drive ahead.

Beside the bar, a long row of truckers idled and coughed puffs of laughter. They took turns staring through a peephole into the restaurant next door. Passively entertained, one laughed and encouraged his comrade to follow him before all of them returned to the tables. Moving as discretely as he imagined thieves capable of doing, Uri walked over and stood next to the peephole bobbing his head to the soulful chain of blues. He waited for his opportunity when he could not feel any of the patron's eyes judging him and went to the hole to see what wonders were on the other side.

He exhaled a stifled gasp as he looked once, then again, then he could not look away. He had never witnessed the spectacle that now chimerically gyrated in front of him. A continuous spectrum of belt buckles danced together in one holy order. Sometimes they stopped together, precipitating a thundering clap of unified hands with such strength that they were never in need of musical percussion. White lights streaked through the smoke and illuminated the large, brass sphere belt buckles that danced only for Uri. Shallow engravings were etched around the buckle's stars and stag bulls and spoke of grand rodeo victories from the past. No one in the room had ever won a rodeo competition. All of them had come to the trucking trade through some calamitous personal or moral reason or another and the buckles were their redemptive fantasy. As long as the deceit was theirs and theirs alone a spoiler's rain need never drop in trucker's paradise.

Uri was utterly transfixed on each dashing flash of metal that appeared before him and then squirted away from the hole like an ancient species of squid that was too noble to ever be catalogued. Uri placed his hand and then his ear on the wall and felt the comfortable country and western pulse that had guided him to The South. The song was muffled, he could not discern the lyrics. He could feel the rhythm in his hand and then he heard the music in his head. It made him ecstatic.

Uri saluted the surly barkeep who responded with a slight nod of his head that he immediately regretted granting to a stranger and then Uri exited and went next door. Under the red neon dog, he looked up into the teeth of the beast and his heart warmed. The door was oak, heavy, and scraped the floor along its well-trod arc as he forced his way through. When he saw what was inside, he wanted to be bedazzled but was not. In a confused panic, he sought out music and the mystical belt-buckles that he had seen dancing in the smoke-filled ether he had known a few ticks of a watch before.

He pressed his hand and ear against the wall and felt the music from the other side. He knew that there must be another room separating him from those dancing belt buckles in the bright stage light. Confused, he continued to feel for the origin of so much wonderment. Immediately, he drew the ferocious attention of the dazed denizens who idly sat for a rest and reprieve from their line dancing.

A group of white truckers with identical and brazen belt buckles sat close to where Uri was conducting his metaphysical investigation. They spoke amongst themselves quietly.

"Hey, Joey, what you make of this guy here." He was a dapper man in his Friday night's best, wearing a modest cowboy hat set atop a subdued plaid so that his belt-buckle would shine even brighter.

"Beats me. Looks like he searching for something—that, or he's in love with the wall."

"Hey, buddy, buddy!"

Uri turned away from the wall.

"Hello, my little friend."

"What you looking for behind that wall there?"

Uri faltered while trying to remember country songs in search of the correct words. It was a gap in his mind like he had been asked to give the date of the most beautiful sunset he had ever seen. "There were many beautiful flying circles of steel. They were here a few moments ago. There were strange writings and big bulls."

The table of men glanced at each other to be absolutely certain that they agreed Uri had misunderstood the exact same thing. And then they laughed.

"Boy, you Northerners got no appreciation for the good things in life. You see this here?" He drew back from the table and displayed his belt buckle that was bordered with shining fake jewels. "This here a genuine championship buckle complete with a custom-made bola." He reached for his neck to show his bola that had been designed with more care than the man's first marriage. "What you Northerners got to compare to that?"

Uri was speechless.

"Where you coming from anyway?"

Uri said, "I'm from Boston."

"Boston? Hell's bells! You the original. Becha your great daddy was throwing away tea while mine was building his first farm. Ain't that right?"

"I do not know."

"No sense of history, eh? That's the problem these days with all the internet and videogames and such. Me, I like to listen to tapes on history while I'm on the road. Given myself a first-rate education after all these years. Have a seat son, pour yourself a pitcher. Darlene? Darlene, baby-cake, another glass over here."

A waitress across the room heard his call and fetched another glass for the table. It arrived before Uri could forget about the belt buckles from a few seconds before.

"I'm Joe, this here Bobby, and this dapper gentleman to your right is Lukas. We're the three musketeers. Ride the road together, live free or die, that type of thing."

"Truck drivers have a very exciting life."

"Well, we do the best we can. What's your name anyway, fella?"

"I'm Uri."

"Maury, eh? Good northern name. You hear that, fellas? This here Maury come all the way from Boston to have a drink at the old Hair of the Dog Saloon. Good times, good times. Here Maury, have a drink." He poured a beer and adroitly removed the pitcher at the decisive moment to prevent foam from flowing over the rim of the glass. "So, Maury, what brings you all the way here from Boston?"

"I was told by a friend that The South was where I should be."

"I know what you mean, you can have the rest of the world. Something 'bout the air here, when I breathe, I know I'm home, know what I mean?" Lukas stroked his hair and wrapped his fingers against the table. He created his own percussion with a thick brass ring that ensconced a large, red, worthless jewel. The newly baptized Maury could not help but notice it and inquire.

"That is a very big ring, where did you get it?"

Lukas looked up and grinned with the sparkle of a patiently unearthed gem. "Football, state champs, blood, sweat, and poontang, my good man. Ain't no feeling like it."

"The ring is very nice and big." Maury quipped back through the escalating volume of the music that triggered an emotional tremor through the table.

"You play sports, Maury?"

"When I was little. I was big so I was good."

"Wonder why you little Northerners never do too good at football, must be all that cold weather and polluted air. Can't grow no roots in all that cement."

The music rose again, reminding Maury of the peephole that had shown him so many wonderful things before vanishing from physical existence. Two members of Joey's three musketeers got up to drink whiskey and relieve their bladders as their bodies almost anticipated the tide of music that was about to arrive. As soon as they left Uri rose in search of the peephole to look to the new other side. His hand caressed the smooth, cold paint and rejoiced under the electric, thumping sensations of the music from beyond the wall. He lovingly placed his ear against the wall and furtively stroked his hand over the cold grain of paint to try and find any opening at all.

His search lasted until the music crescendoed again and the bar reached a new height of invigoration. When Maury discovered the peephole, he was happy and alarmed by a painful wail on the other side when his finger popped the eye of an anonymous voyeur who then identified himself with a screech of obscenity, punctuated by tossing the ice from his cognac into the hole and the inquisitive face of Uri who was investigating the cause of the chaos. The cognac spurted through with the delayed natural pop of a whale clearing water from its blowhole. Uri staggered back to the table he had been sitting at before. The men were gone as they had risen together like a church congregation to go dancing. Joe noticed Maury and moved through the crowd towards him in awkward strides as his belt buckle's size impeded normal motion.

"Maury, Maury, you OK, what happened?"

Maury raised his hand and pointed to the peephole in the wall. Joe went to investigate and saw nothing.

"No, here, I took the drink in the face here." Maury rose to show him and poked the hole with his finger with the begrudging condescension of a magician revealing the mechanics of his livelihood. Maury thrust his finger in and out, waiting to feel something on the other side.

"Son of a bitch." Joe bent down and gazed into the other restaurant. By now the rest of his comrades had circled around he and Maury.

"What's the matter, Joe?"

"What's going on? I love this song." Joe stood, somber and proud, the eyes and concentration of his friends riveted to him before proclaiming,

"Them coons been spying on us." He then turned to lean on the wall, exhausted from his own exacerbation.

"What you mean Joe?

"Yeah, Joe, what you saying? Why ain't you dancing?" Joe tipped his cowboy hat deeply over his eyes.

"Look, will yah fellahs, just look." Joe stuck his finger through the hole as Maury had done. His friends bent over to look through and confirm what Joe's fingers had already known.

"Son of a bitch. Joe, those coons been spying on us."

"I know, I know." Joe patted him on the back, nearly embracing him but not quite.

"What we gonna do now? I can't dance with them watching. Can't show off my rodeo pride with all them on the other side sniggering and pointing. What we gonna do?"

"I say we cover it up, and slash all their tires, that teach them a lesson." Lukas said while fidgeting with the bowie knife he had artfully concealed in his boot.

"Nah, we can't do nothing like that, we can't cover it up, then they win." Joe defeatedly said, his voice wavering.

"What you mean we can't cover it up?" Lukas argued. Joe thought before speaking in a rising helix of rage and pride.

"We can't cover it up 'cause we got nothing to be ashamed of. Look at us, just a bunch of good old boys having a good time, now here we are, all upset cause a bunch of coons staring at us and laughing. We got nothing to be ashamed of, but we do got our pride so we gotta think of something. We got the jump on those bastards now; they don't know that we know. We got the jump on them now, so I say we go and put those big ol' Harvard thinking hats on and come up with some way to get them back and get them good." He paused for a moment and looked into the future "All right, boys, fuck it, I ain't in the dancing mood no more, let's get back and get some sleep. Hey, Maury, where you staying?"

Maury thought to himself and of his car. "I don't know. Where are you staying?" He sighed, critiquing himself for some faux pas he could not express.

"We all staying at a little hotel for truckers and the like, not the greatest place for you city-slickers, but we like it. You wanna come? It's cheap as dirt and I know the manager so maybe I get you to sleep there for free."

"Yes, that sounds good, I will follow your big trucks."

"Why you gotta talk like that, sure as hell follow up the convoy. The way the west was won and all that, OK fellas swallow your drinks whole, we'll get those coons back another night."

They all finished their beer with one deft chug and all exited in a row. Joe waited in the back and waved his hat to the bar and mouthed the words adios muchachos until his favorite waitress that he would never fuck acknowledged him and waved goodbye.

The drive to the transient hotel was somber for Maury no matter how loudly he played his optimistic country songs into the sweet Georgia night. He missed his name. Boston, New York, Europe, all his homes were all blurred. Every day he fell in love with some great new thing that was embedded in the soul of these people's boring, normal, forgettable moments. Maury warred with the country song, he spoke his old Czech name to himself: Jiří. The foreign shape of the tongue already altered by the numb vowels of so many stories he had played in his car and in his head until the core of that person he used to know so intimately had given way to the undefinable.

That person was somewhere in the briar of culture and so many languages, so many that he never really had a mother tongue. Words like *armpit* would vanish from his memory, lost in the nuanced roman scripts of a continent.

"My name is Jiři." He said it again and again. "I am from Europe, and I am to want find adventure American, you great imperialist, great emperor bastard, Yankee go home." He was now screaming above and against the country western music. He could smell the net of security that he had known in Europe vanish and he suddenly believed that not having any money made every step of his unwise and that Europe missed him. Europe, that one big bickering family missed him. He believed that the Americans were a different thing entirely who were driven towards ends that never made sense, but always greatness. That was the result, that was the light they saw in their bleakest days: greatness, a nation of emerging geniuses battling their own self-imposed obscurity. He believed all these things until the truck in front of him signaled to turn off the freeway and he again put his sorrow away and joined, believing too that his soul was a moment of greatness that had yet to emerge. It was the belief that might carry him west in the way of all Americans who earn their mythology.

The midnight moon cast a sedentary glance over *Howard's Trucker's Motel*. Maury looked to the flickering sign with its billowing light and wondered about the grammar of the name. His eyes probed through the night. Everything seemed so overwhelmingly vast. Two lines of three-storied barracked housing separated by an expansive sea of asphalt. The entire complex was adjacent to a filthy diner evoking the aesthetics of the 1950's. It was named merely Merv's, spelled out in flickering, broken-neon cursive. Merv's had been run by the same family of men for three generations and all of them lived and died unmarried while finding the rare occasion to impregnate one of the prostitutes that lingered in the restaurant between shifts in the truck motel.

The motel offered hourly rates, but this was considered rude to take according to local custom, so all parties involved insisted on a one-night commitment. This social contract had created a stable economy between the two establishments for three generations. The faces and races of management changed, yet the gushing impetus of business never ceased. Truckers and whores convened under the candle-like halo of neon for a sliver of connection in between so many miles of serpentine asphalt that separated the men from their other human connections.

Maury found a place to park in the back away from the long spaces reserved for the trucks. He met the trio at their trucks while they were cleaning their lips of stinging wads of chewing tobacco and lighting up cigarettes. Every man had pride in his own brand that he chose to distinguish himself from the others in the group.

"Well Maury, welcome to Atlanta, Georgia, the bright shining queen of The South. Say that's bout right fellas." They all mumbled in agreement. "Now, if you look there, past that truck and tween those buildings you can make out the skyline of the city. Pretty ain't it." Maury squinted to bring more detail to the tuft of gray buildings standing out in all that night.

"Do you go there?" Maury asked.

"Nah, it's for city folks. We're just good old Southern boys. Can't afford it or think through it, so I say fuck it, eh fellas?" A contagious chuckle bounced through the group. "It just don't feel right in there, like everybody trying to be something they not, like they forgot what Atlanta means, forgot its history, y'know. It ain't 'bout all the razzle dazzle, but about The South, you understand?"

"I think so, a people need a history."

"Exactly, and you can't just go and write it away with all them checks like they trying to do, they ain't Georgia and they ain't the south. They just little baby New Yorkers who ain't never gonna grow up, only grow old. Y'know what I mean? Well, you from Boston, you probably get it."

"Oh yes, I think."

"Ah enough of this, the fellas and myself got a little tradition, we all going over to Merv's over there get a little burger and boogie before bed, I know you new in town, but I figure you probably in it for a new experience, right? And believe you me, there ain't nothing like Merv's. I'll just go get us checked in, see if I can't get you a key too, Maury." Joe walked over to the illuminated box where the clerk sat reading a copy of *National Geographic*. Joe was disappointed that it was not pornography because now they would have very little to discuss during check-in except their own lives.

"How long you think you'll be staying here in Georgia?" Lukas asked Maury while offering a half-pack of Pall Malls that he accepted out of nostalgia and politeness.

"I do not know; I came here for an adventure. Whenever the wind blows me to Texas, like the song says."

"What song is that?" Bobby asked curiously.

"I do not remember, the man was big, in a black hat, he really loved the Texas."

"Shit, could be just 'bout anyone then." Lukas spoke through his own drunken snorts, a habit of his he had never noticed because no one would ever tell him, "Just 'bout every hillbilly loves Texas, can't stand the fucking place myself, bunch of little dick peckers thinking that they cross the Louisiana border they fall off the edge of the world."

"Why the hell you going to Texas?" Bobby was drunk and becoming angry and very concerned for Maury's future.

"It was just in the song."

"You think that all us bumpkins down here a part of Texas, like Texas ain't big enough?"

"Bobby, calm down and shut the fuck up, the man's on his great adventure from the north, course he gonna hit Texas, how can he miss it? First thing though, if you have to leave Georgia, and that's a big if, I think you might like it, but if you have to you got to go to New Orleans. My Grand pappy's got a little place down there, won't mind the company neither. Hell, probably won't know the difference." They shared a laugh and another cigarette when Joe returned with four keys.

"Got one for you for free, Maury, good people here, very good people. Now, I got a hankering for one of them Merv's burgers and you know what else, let's see what the cat drug in. C'mon Maury, welcome to The South." With a pat on the shoulder and a bounce in his step, Joe guided Maury and his friends over to Merv's while regaling him with exciting tales of when the trio had been there before. The stories were hysterical and changed each time he told them. Variations on a constant theme instead of a concrete memory and as he would note as the night stretched longer and thinner: who would want a steel trap memory anyway? Means nothing can get away.

The crowd at Merv's was a bevy of midnight workers and working-day prostitutes. Maury looked to the sign for neon guidance and found none and then ventured inside behind Joe and his gang. The bar bustled with the smell of food good only in the early crevices of the morning and the scent of the commerce of human flesh. A mixture of baby powder and imitation perfumes that osmotically absorbs the wages of so many married men. They were greeted by a buxom black woman with a shimmering smile that seemed out of place in the early morning light of grizzled potatoes and simmering bacon.

"Hey, Joe, haven't seen you in a while, passing through again or you decided to settle down and make some kids for your mamma?"

"Enough of that, Jeanie. Just here for the night, but this here little traveler might be staying for a while, thinking 'bout giving Atlanta a try, ain't you, Maury?"

"I certainly am. I was born a country boy—I think."

Joe slapped Maury with a generous guffaw and an iron clasp on the shoulder. "Don't mind him, Jeanie, he's from Boston."

"Good lord, you come a long way. You want your usual booth, Joe? Just opened up, I suspect on account that they heard you coming." She winked at him and grabbed four menus. "Right this way, y'all." When they were seated at the booth Maury ran his hand over the cool formica covering that was coated with a perpetually shining gloss. It was the same pattern as the floor, only a different color.

"Well, Maury, you in for a treat, the place is jumping tonight, look at all these little chick-a-dees lined up in a row." Across from the booth were seated twelve prostitutes, one for each chair. They were sipping coffee and picking through scrambled eggs. "You see that Maury, you can have any one of those ladies, two, but it'll cost you more, any one of those ladies, ain't America sweet? Bet you can't find this in Boston. You ever been to a place like this in Boston?"

"No, I have never seen anything like this. This is for country boys."

"Nah, this is for good old boys, country boys something else. See, if you was a country boy you'd take that fat dark skinned one on the end. See her, not smiling or nothing, wonder how she stays employed? Fuck it all. Let's get something to eat. That whiskey's sitting in my stomach and it's hungrier than me." The prostitutes sat and idly chatted amongst themselves while the humming florescent lights made them appear as tired as they actually were despite the best efforts of makeup to conceal the consequences of hard lives lived in excess. Neat, dirty clothes clung to their flesh. They had not been laundered in a long time, yet they kept their erotic allure. The prostitutes did not look askance or saunter through the thin isles linked to booths of half-giddy, half-deranged truckers. The entire restaurant obeyed a type of elementary school decorum. Everyone remained seated and watched one another while waiting for the correct time to leave.

A waitress with authentic insomnia approached the table and removed her pen from her large greasy bun knotted atop her head. Joe said that they needed more time to order. She waited patiently, casting an irritated glare over everyone with each slow blink until Joe spoke up for all of them and ordered, "Ah, hell, we'll all get the special, that egg sausage deal, scramble them puppies, you can do that can't you, sug?"

"Anything Joe wants." She removed the menus with short stabbing motions and replaced her pen into her hair before scurrying back to the kitchen behind metallic doors, having never written anything. Maury stared at the doors that swung in and out three pulsing times before closing behind the waitress. The row of prostitutes did not stir. Nor did they finish their food. They sat and sipped coffee without end. Maury sniffed the air and watched.

"What do you think so far, Maury? Pretty wild stuff, city folk don't get this, they don't understand, all them fellas go to the titty bars and spend all their money, don't even get a reach around on their gay-old-daisy-train, know what I mean?" Joe paused to reflect, Lukas and Bob nodded their heads in staunch agreement, like listening to a persuasive politician explain why poverty was a necessary and correct thing in the world. "Now, these here ladies, these here, they don't charge by the hour or nothing like that, I don't know why city folk even bother. I got a cousin-in-law working the belly of Atlanta, does a lot of lawyering stuff, now he was telling me he pays his girls by the hour. Imagine that? I can't. No way, not for good old Joe here, these girls willing to spend the night with you, cause they grateful, just the way a woman should be, they happy to get a few ten spots and a shower, know what I mean? Charging by the hour, what the hell is that? I mean, we all men here, we got needs, the Bible knows that, but if you gotta fuck a whore, best it doesn't feel like prostitution. I mean, I can't imagine Lukas here working his magic and all the while she looking at her watch like it's about to be quitting time."

The waitress arrived with the food steaming uncomfortably on her arm. Maury noticed that she had developed thin, coarse calluses along her forearm in a row of vague crescents lined up from the hot plates she ported to the tables every night. Joe was ecstatic to eat and to speak. Suddenly, the world entered a divine order through the prism of his eyes. He grabbed the waitress with his voice as she turned to walk away from their table and onto the next. "Say, baby, doll face." The waitress stopped without showing her indignation at the realization that no one had addressed her by her Christian name in over a year, except for her mother with nascent Alzheimer's, but those phone calls from the home had ceased as of late. The phone became a terrifying thing for her mother and for the strangers she haphazardly dialed, screaming at them like the lovers from her twenties she thought they were.

The waitress had stopped believing she was only working here until something better would come along. She envied other cultures that never granted the delusion of upward mobility to the next generation.

Joe continued, "Sugar cakes, what time's your shift get over? Maybe you'd like to get a big, hot cup of Joe when you done with work?" She blinked twice to ensure he had finished and proceeded to speak.

"I sleep in the back of the kitchen because I couldn't live across the parking lot no more, no how. The sound of you fucking a whore every time you pass through was keeping me awake, so I reckon that I'll be going to sleep in the kitchen, back there, away from you, and away from all the whores. Thank you." She pivoted with sloppy cavalcade steps and retreated behind the kitchen doors.

"Is she a joking woman?" Maury asked.

"Hell, I don't know. Women like that don't joke. Life ain't too funny after they been fucked too much. Kind of a weird balance thing. But she ain't no Southern belle neither, and that's good—real good. You best watch for them Southern belles. Most manipulative women in the world. They'll have you married and two feet in the grave while you tie their daddy's shoe in the blink of an eye. Blink of an eye, Maury! I'm telling you. No Southern belles, little sugar tush back there might be a bit feisty, but she the closest thing to an honest woman you gonna find in these parts—except for my beautiful baby sitting over there. Get a good look, Maury."

One of the prostitutes individuated herself from the crowd by staring intensely at Joe while he sloppily devoured his eggs and coffee. "Look at that, Maury. She ordered the same thing, eggs and coffee, a woman after my own heart. Hell."

Maury looked at his food and everyone's food and saw that it was all identical. "But Joe, everyone here is eating . . ."

"Shhh, shhh, shhh." Joe ducked his head under the brim of his hat to surreptitiously look at the girl who was staring directly through him. "Sweet Josephine has laid an egg, and that's my bird for the night. Ooowee, Maury. Hey, Lukas, Bob, think she got some friends for us?"

"I don't know, Joe, I definitely take seconds on her. You got yourself a widdle puddy-cat there."

"Hell, Lukas, they all interested in you, just gotta have confidence man, that's what these chicks dig, it's the confidence man."

"I don't know, Joe. Hey, Maury, how this compare to that Boston pussy?" Maury looked to Lukas and thought of his last lover, a French girl with a crescent scar across her stomach from where her stillborn child had been removed. Recalling the beauty of the moment, he then kept it to himself.

"These girls seem much friendlier and sexier dressers, no thick sailor coats."

"Here's to the Georgia peach, nicer than The South, but just as sweet." The coffee cups violently clanged in the middle of the table, swapping fluids before the four men quietly sat and tried to return the passionate gaze beamed on them from the row of women.

"Fuck y'all cowards, I'm going in." Joe adjusted his hat and looked at his reflection on the back of his dirty fork, straightening his eyebrows through floating bits of scrambled eggs. "Well boys, cover me. We'll meet later at tango bravo." Joe adjusted his hat so the brim would stare directly into the eyes of his girl and walked over to the counter. As Joe approached, the prostitute gave the woman next to her the slightest twitch of her pinkie finger, and she immediately evacuated the seat without looking at Joe.

He asked, "Hey, sugar baby, this seat taken?"

"It's taken by you, daddy-o."

He chuckled and looked back to his friends who eagerly gesticulated their support, giving him confidence. He winked back to them to let them know that he was in charge of the situation.

"So, tell me, what's a beautiful lady like you doing at a little old dump like this, eating eggs during Satan's witching hour of night?"

"Well, I don't quite know, sug, I reckon that I'm just waiting for my prince charming."

Lukas and Bobby gazed and guffawed with eager eyes while Maury just stared, confused.

"Man, that Joe is the man, he gonna get us all ladies tonight."

"Yeah, you know pretty girls like that, always have prettier friends they don't show cause of the female jealousy thing." Joe continued speaking and the prostitute stroked his face and lifted his hat while brushing her fingers through his greasy hair. Tenderly, she leaned into him, and with soft breaths, said something preternaturally alluring and then smiled to the trio at the table, slithering her tongue through the hole in her mouth where two teeth had been violently knocked out. She still kept those teeth huddled together in her purse and would feel them between her pinkie and thumb from time to time.

"Man, look at her, look at those teeth. She a mean one."

"Shut up, Bobby. I think she's a sweetheart, a good old gal not stuck on herself."

"That Joe always been magic with the ladies."

"Sure has Bobby, weehee, we all getting laid tonight." Maury looked to his two companions and then back to Joe before speaking.

"I am very sorry, and I have many apologies for offending you, but that woman is a prostitute correct?"

"Sure as sunshine on shit, she is." Lukas retorted, never looking away.

"And Joe will pay her to have sex with him?"

"Sure will. Her friends, too. Don't worry, he won't leave you out, you'll get yours."

"Yes, I see, but the thing I am wondering is, why is there this romance? Why meet in a café? The truckers are sleeping over there." He waved his hand to the outside world.

"Shit, boy, you Northerners can't do nothing right. You gotta have a little romance. We all sailing this sea of shit together, been on the road for a long time, need a little people time, y'know what I'm saying? Last thing anybody wants is to feel like they paying for sex, feel like prostitution, feel like you gotta pay some big ass negro pimp in a fur coat half your money plus a tip so he keep the skanks away from you. Damn, boy, no wonders you ain't been living."

"Yeah, Lukas is right. I agree, man. Now, I don't want to sound like a fag or nothing, but when I'm with a lady, I don't like feeling that she fucking me for cash. That's just wrong, it's dirty and it's wrong, that much is in the Bible."

"I understand. The South is a different thinking of life."

"Bet your sweet ass, city boy. Now take a look, Joe 'bout to make his move." On the stool, Joe finally submitted and put his arm around his prostitute. She smiled and he laughed. Her hot breath cast a spell into his ear. His torso twisted with the chair, and he called his compatriots over to the row. Lukas and Bobby were quickly paired with the two women next to Joe's prostitute while Maury stood aloof, curious, and concerned.

"So, what you ladies think? You got another little filly friend for this here Maury who come all the way from Boston?"

"My, they grow them so very tall up north, don't they?" Joe's prostitute was the leader of the other two. She had a raspy old voice because her larynx had been scraped by too many cigarette draws and pulls of whiskey.

"Well, what do you say darling? You got something for Maury here." Joe was euphoric. The prostitute at the end, the small one with Bobby, piped in and was immediately shushed by a look from her leader. "We are a trio, like sisters, the three amigas." Joe's girl looked dolorously at the shortest and youngest girl.

"What my small piece of sug there is trying to say is that we work together, watching over the interests of the other and such, but he should try Patricia down there at the end."

"Oh no, mister, I heard . . ." The small one started to pipe in.

"You heard nothing that I don't already know. Go give her a try, I heard she likes Northerners." She turned back to Joe's lap and fed him her finger, whispering into his ear.

"Yup, sug. That sounds just fine by me. Maury, you gonna be ok here?"

"Yes, I will talk to Patricia and learn Southern romance."

"Eheh. Southern romance. This boy be all right, eh, sugar pop?"

"Yes, he is certainly not one of us. C'mon boys." The six of them filed out of the building. On the way out, the shortest and youngest prostitute slapped Bobby below his belt to jettison him out of the door. She then snuck in close to Maury, sexually clung to him, and said, "Be careful, mister. Patricia been touched, that's what I heard. Bye."

Maury leaned over so that she could kiss him on the cheek. "Take care, little creature."

She scurried away into the night, exiting with the screeching metal sound of the door that had been ready to come unhinged for years.

Maury felt his key in his pocket and thought of that lumpy bed waiting for him that was so much better than inside the car. Then there was Patricia. He patted the key to his room.

The counter before him seemed to stretch out to a longer and longer distance. Anticipating the bliss of discovery, he approached Patricia, the woman at the end, accosted by no one. She sat and simply sipped her coffee on the outskirt of a row of whores. A frame of tranquil beauty in repose. He sat beside her and looked to the haggard waitress and asked her for a menu as if he had just arrived. She rolled her eyes and handed him the menu. The menu was stuck together with the lacquered remnants of so many prepackaged doses of jam and syrup. It released a prolonged squeal as he opened it. He read the menu and relished each strange noun that he understood in new ways after his jagged immersion into country-western English. 'Lumber Jack's Specials' and 'Trucker's Rig' emerged in bold epiphanies and Maury chuckled as he now knew exactly who they were speaking about.

"I reckon these'll all look pretty good for my baby." He realized how softly he was speaking and pushed the throttle of his pronunciation until the entire row of prostitutes became alerted to his presence and either scowled or emitted a cardsharp's slanting grin.

"Don't play yourself so hard, big daddy. I ain't the lady for you."

Maury ordered a coffee and smiled as he knew another adventure awaited him—he was certain of it. "Yes? How do you know?"

"You're too young for me."

"But I am grown man. See? Mustache." He pointed to the tuft of hair jettisoning from his lip. Embarrassed, he groomed the hairs until they had a curvaceous quality that women in Europe had appreciated before.

"Trust me, you're too young for my kind of love. But I'd love one of those cigarettes." She turned her hips to him and revealed droopy eyes.

"How do you know I smoke?"

"Your accent. Now, are you gonna treat me like a lady or what?"

Cautiously searching his own pockets, he found the half-empty pack of Pall Malls and sighed in relief. Patricia reached into her purse and unveiled a 99-cent lighter inserted into a case of gold plastic gilded with fake rubies. Aggressively, Maury grabbed it from her hand and excitedly inhaled the flame through the waiting tobacco. He had felt some prohibition against smoking his entire time in America. He now relished the chance to shatter a taboo with each nicotine-infused inhalation.

"Been a while, huh? Maybe you need a new drug. Hate to see another cigarette junkie roaming the streets of Atlantis."

Maury exhaled in religious gratitude. "Atlantis? Where is this? I want to go."

She eyed him with maternal affection and snorted. "Doesn't really exist, just a name for something that I don't think was ever there. Can't imagine it anyway."

"Atlantis. I like the name, it's fun to say, Atlantis. Yes." He ordered another coffee and more eggs.

"You seem far too interesting to be here. What's your story?"

"I am here for my adventure."

"I see. And that's how you met Joe? Adventure?"

"Joe is a good guy."

"Yup, a good old boy, used to be a rare thing, a hard thing to be, hard lives lived by hard men, now it's every yahoo behind the wheel of a sixteen-wheeler is a good old boy. Christ. But yeah, Joe all right, I guess."

"And you, do you have a story?"

"I'm a woman, I have many."

"Are they all good?"

"Nah, pretty depressing stuff. I'm kind of retired from the game—so to speak. Now, I'm just going to sit here until Mr. Right comes through that door, and then that'll be the last seduction."

"Then you will get married?"

"Whatever he wants, doesn't really matter to me."

"How do you know he will be here?" Shyly intrigued he continued. "And how do you know it is not me?"

She smiled and stroked his face with a porcelain hand bleached by jagged scars over her fingers. "I told you sug, you're too young for me. As for how I know he'll be here, let's just say I had a sign and this little Southern belle ain't moving until he comes. We each have a destiny and mine is in that other person."

"You think God wants you to meet your white knight in this diner."

"God is done with me. I just have my destiny, and between us little chickens here that is none of His fucking business."

Maury liked her, the fact that she told him that he could not even pay her for sex and allowed him to smoke cigarette after cigarette relaxed him to the point of trust and they sat like two bewildered children and watched the depraved machinations of the diner as it routed the sex trade bereft of pimps through haggard waitresses and syndicates of like-minded junkies of heroine, meth, and flesh. All of it on the outskirts of Atlanta just out of reach of high urban money while rife with the gravity of urbanity's failings.

Verse 2

aury awoke to Joe's dulcet pounding on his door. The mattress beneath reminded him that he was alive with an exotic form of the uncomfortable. There had been mattresses he despised before in every crevice of Europe, bags of lumpy lumps that invaded his muscles and wounded him for the day. This was different as the mattress was thin and sallow and never resisted his weight. Occasional silver metal springs burst through the fabric to prick his flesh like mushrooms that mysteriously appear after a dark night. Maury rose and opened the door to see Joe smiling and bobbing from too much coffee.

"Ooooohhhhhweee boy, you get lucky last night?" Maury's eyes blinked and he looked behind Joe for meaning and found none.

"I, I don't understand." Joe pushed Maury aside and looked at the empty, speckled mattress.

"Now, that is a shame. Feel bad getting so much for old Joe and nothing for little Maury here. Tell you what, me and the boys gotta head out now, but we be back in about a month. I just checked my schedule and around then we set to go to New Orleans. You never been to old Nawlins now, have you?"

"Not in this life."

"Hehehe, yeah, guess we can all say that from time to time, anyway, you stick around here, and I'll pick you up to go on down in one month if you still around. If you move on out just leave a note with the desk; they real friendly and always been good to old Joe. It's a deal, all right?" He extended his hand to Maury's and firmly shook it. "Be seeing you now, until that day." With a tip of his hat, he jubilantly cavorted down the long, cement balcony while clanging the iron stairs on his descent with his aging and immortal boots.

The parking lot was now flush with travelers of The South. Prostitutes emerged from the rooms and faintly pulled their clothing into order on the balconies while waving across the parking lot to their sisters in arms. Joe's truck pulled strenuously through Maury's vision and released a billowing pull of the horn that ricocheted between the buildings. Everyone else had awakened with a compulsion to leave. The sun crested and shattered the shadow of the awning above to cast Maury into a blinding morning light and only then did he feel the nature of his indecency. He was clad only in a stale pair of boxers that he decided to retire in that moment with a great degree of sadness. They were the triggering mechanism for so many memories he would otherwise never recall. They had stayed with him longer than any lover and now they seemed too dirty and fatigued to endure the rigor The South was certain to bring.

Maury showered in the darkened bathroom and emerged tingling with the pulse of the new day and new adventure. He stopped to stare deeply into a mirror and with a smile reminded himself gleefully that this was America. He had no history to interpret, no past to remember, and only a European life to forget.

All of it was trapped in the memories of other people, discarded lovers, and outgrown friends. Without the connection of a relationship and without another set of eyes from which to share life everything would be forgotten like the morning's reflection. Maury was free to be born every day a new soul fresh from the shower. He had his freedom if only he could remember to forget the daily continuity of that face that stared back from the mirror.

He stepped back outside his room. The hazy sun blurred the parking lot and transformed the diner across the street into a monolithic mirage. Maury smiled and reflected on the previous night when a guttural arrow of sound pierced through the air and laced his ears. Instinctively, he strained to make it out. It was something from his past, something he knew by birth and now by instinct. Beneath Maury a group of Russians and Pols were speaking to and through each other in two separate groups. They were arguing and rolling their languages with tongues bereft of the awkward and long vowels he was trying to learn. He smiled and wondered if there was a country western star in Russia. Feeling a tinge of pain and an island of his childhood below, he bounded down the stairs and encountered about a dozen men. All were smoking and drinking and complaining of the new world where only cash is king, and all so far from home without a wife to hold.

Maury begged the group for a moment to introduce himself. They all paused, astonished, holding their bated breaths except for the tough Russians in the back who had seen so many tragic accidents that they would not even be surprised at their own deaths the next year in the silly, screeching machinations of a large American machine deployed to expand a parking lot. Maury said hello and that he was eager to hear the creation story of what had brought so many Slavs to a transient motel on the outskirts of Atlanta.

"Walmart," a few replied with steel in their voices. The most garrulous of the gaggle was also the weakest and so he was the one designated to speak to Maury and tell him of how they all came to be together.

The narratives were indistinct. They were all Slavs who were not intelligent or savage enough to succeed in their homeland. They had all come to America legally and stayed in fear of deportation after the first plume of smoke licked the sky on 9/11. Northern ports of entry had given way to Southern weather. They all wanted to feel the steady heat of the sun against their clothes, stick their tongues out in cool southern mornings and taste the wildly humid air before the first tint of pollution. They were happy upon arrival until the money ran out and they needed warm water, stale beds, and a place to call home. That is when Walmart dragged them all together as the gravity of its size and opportunity was too much to ignore.

Maury had a habit of constantly patting his wallet like a nervous tick that made him feel safe from robbers and flush with cash. In America when he patted his wallet, he felt the terror of the future he had so far successfully ignored. He needed more scraps of paper with dead American presidents stamped across the top. In his life he had lived under the subtle rule of a lot of dead heads of dead presidents. When his mother looked her most stunning, she would go to the borders of East and West, North and South, all the variegated colors of Europe and return with wonderful currencies from across the continent. Some she kept and others she immediately sent away. Even then, Maury's mother would flourish one bill and say that it would buy a house in the bottom of China and another bill would buy the death of a poor man. These bills here, these, she pointed to a stack of British pounds, well these would buy someone's life away from cancer in America. His child eyes filled with ocean-blue wonderment as the power of life and death, right or wrong, could all be found in the small space within a piece of paper. Now, Maury felt the fire of his adventure dwindling under the tales of these men and he knew that his next quest would be to become employed.

One man from the group passed him a bottle of Vodka and asked Maury if he liked it and he said that he did. Then the next man asked Maury if he needed money and Maury said yes.

That night Maury would walk through the aluminum arches of an air-conditioned door and into a service entrance where he would gaze in ceaseless wonderment at a labyrinthine storeroom and come to know the awe and dehumanizing splendor that is Walmart.

Verse 3

It was midnight exactly when The Supervisor approached. He was a tired and fat and everything on his face was disheveled but for a rusty mustache that he fastidiously trimmed almost to the size of Hitler's, almost. The Slavs spread as he approached. The only person who looked The Supervisor directly in the eye was Maury and so he was immediately tagged as the newest shining stone to be cracked and polished by the grinding ax of The Supervisor's corporate moral statement of the day.

"And who might you be?" The Supervisor moved towards Maury and again all moved out of his way all except Maury who suddenly found the height and lights of the ceiling to be a far more interesting thing than the shorter man before him huffing stale breaths of beer. "Your name son, what's the matter, can't speaky-ze-English?"

Like a doll animated to life by an unseen hand Maury replied, "My name is Maury. I am from New York. It is nice to meet you and make your acquaintance."

The Supervisor blinked twice to assure he was conscious. "What are you doing here?"

"I came to work."

"You got a weird accent, you Russian?"

"No, I am from New York."

"You a Jew? You got a weird accent. You one of those New York liberal Jews?"

"I do not think so, my family lost its history in the war."

"Oh, so you ain't an American?"

"Not by birth, no."

"Well then, you got the job."

"Thank you very much."

The Supervisor backed up and placed his hands at his side. Then, as if they were musicians in a symphony about to be led by a conductor, all the Slavs lined up in regimented rows and respectfully placed their hands behind their backs. Maury did so as well but out of sync and out of time. The Supervisor prattled about guidelines and work reviews and then shepherded them into their nightly duty while he privately counted the days before their deportations. While The Supervisor spoke, he acutely felt his deep longing for a promotion to the day shift when at long last he would move from ordering foreigners around to bossing the blacks. Walmart would be good to him in that way. Walmart would give him his chance. He smiled and thought of his bright future in front of an all-black cleaning crew and paced back and forth and rubbed his head looking for the hat of Bear Bryant. When he entered Walmart, he changed between being a lower-middle class man with a wife and lower-class problems to the God of this playing field. Night was when he shined under the hums of the thousands of fluorescent lights that kept Walmart safe.

"OK men, you did an OK job yesterday, but I know you can do better, I want you working hard tonight to make this store shine, you get me boys? I don't want you cleaning and shelving like a bunch of little girls. I want the shelves ordered and the floors shining. I want to walk around the store and see my face shine in every linoleum square, you got me, well, do you? Hey, new guy." He walked right into the face of Maury, "Yeah, I'm talking to you, I think that you don't have what it takes to work for Walmart, I think that you don't have the balls." The rest of the Slavs forgot to laugh.

"Sir, I don't think that I understand."

"What, what don't you understand?"

"What this thing is you want me to do?"

"I don't want you to do a goddamn thing. I asked you a very simple question. Do you have the balls to work for Walmart?" Maury paused and looked to one of his Slavic cohorts, but they stared blankly and exhaustedly forward as they were too accustomed to the inevitable to care anymore.

"Um . . . yes."

"Good goddamn answer Einstein." He backed away from Maury and again started pacing at the front of the men. "Boy, I gotta tell you, if I had a choice between working with a bunch of communists and working with a bunch of niggers, I'd have to say that I would pray for the niggers, and I don't want that to be the case. My daddy don't want that neither, and his daddy sure as Goddamn hell don't want that. So, I'm gonna give you Rusky bastards one more chance to prove yourself to me, you hear me? We gonna start the night out right and work hard until dawn and then you can go out and get some of that fire water Russian vodka shit and I won't replace you all with a bunch of niggers, how that sound to you boys?"

Suddenly, and in unison, the entire cadre, except Maury, chanted, "Sounds goddamn good to me, sir!"

The Supervisor continued. "Good, that's what I want to hear. Now, let's bow our heads and sing the Walmart song."

Half of the Slavs immediately began singing, "WE LOVE WALMART. YES WE DO. WE LOVE WALMART. HOW ABOUT YOU?", then the other half paused, drew a communal breath together and responded with more fire, "WE LOVE WALMART. YES WE DO. WE LOVE WALMART. HOW ABOUT YOU?" The Supervisor stood before them all, conducting his symphony of compliance. He was deep inside himself riding waves of bliss. To Maury, it sounded like a swan song with a corporate logo that was building towards oblivion. The chorus continued and increased to fevered crescendos until the voices of the Slavs had almost reached their screeching end. The Supervisor felt this and raised his arms in Episcopal ecstasy after the last counter-song from the Slavs on his right. They were singing into his good ear. In the last lacuna all sucked a breath and then together they sang with military enthusiasm, "WE LOVE WALMART. YES WE DO. WE LOVE WALMART THROUGH AND THROUGH." Then the hands of The Supervisor rested, and all were still and breathless.

"Good job boys, I'll be in my office." He turned his back to them and stormed into a glass box.

The Slavs stayed at attention longer than The Supervisor wanted so he stood at his office door, "What are you damn communists waiting for? The French to come and give you welfare? Get to work." He smiled and they scattered to their designated posts. The jobs had all been distributed according to nationality. The Russians, the true ones, who suffered like Russians and were too poor to have ever seen Moscow remained in the back under the lazily watching eye of The Supervisor. He thought that it would be harder for them to steal if they were in the back. The other Slavs: The Polskas, Belorussians, Ukrainians, Czechs, and the obligatory Croat shuffled into the front of the store to claim their mops and get to work. Their common language was Russian, and it was one that Maury did not speak.

Thick rubber doors stolidly gave way to the slow-motion janitors entering a vast realm of florescence and novelty. Maury scanned it all in a sublime flash. He saw the never-spoiling food that would keep for years. How long would the moisture in a Snicker's candy bar remain sealed in plastic? Then the potato chips. He fondled the bags like an adolescent who has discovered courage with a girl for the very first time. He slowly uttered brand names. New words, new English phrases on the bag. Expressions that made no grammatical sense but that he needed to understand.

There was one in particular he would never forget: *Once you pop, you can't stop*. Marvelous. Then his eyes moved to the guns, and he glanced further, fascinated and appalled. Beneath the glass case were the tools of rage and fire. Fascinating. He looked behind at the neatly aligned boxes holding the bullets. The whole setup felt like a bar for Maury. Walk right up and glance down at the menu over the cheap beers and then the mixed drinks and then the scotch that he could never afford, but maybe someday. That scotch aged in oak, the same oak of the stock of the 12-gauge shotgun smiling back at him with its empty barrel. He would then ask the barkeep for some bullets, the type to feed his aggression. He would look at them and reflect and think of the imaginary wife who bore a child too stupid to his liking and then becoming too fat for his taste. He would think of those things and shove the bullet into its rightful place within the chamber. The steel click of a thrust of the hand would ensure him that it was loaded and ready for wife or burglar, child or friend. America was teaching him that there was no such thing as chance. Destiny was an American thing *and* the result of constant hard work.

His eyes put the guns down and moved to the electronics and other media. The history of the world on discounted DVD's. *Spartacus, Braveheart, Gladiator, Lord of the Rings*. His favorite. The only film to ever capture the spirit of Europe and the seeds of its destruction. He looked to the guns and then to the movies. He then looked for a section selling whiskey to complete all the bridges of his American fantasy. You hold the gun and you feel the power, you must, anyone would, you drink the whiskey and watch the film. Then you become something else, the hero, something far greater than a clerk in a store or cubicle ant. You do these things; you combine guns and alcohol and cinema, and you become something greater. At least for shimmering moments, and that was fine, because that's what comprised him. He felt guns, whiskey, and cinema combine and his soul began to grow. He was coming to understand the world through a different lens.

He longed for alcohol and wondered aloud why any American would need to leave Walmart and was curious if the company offered apartments to rent somewhere in the ceiling above the soft and maddening glare of so much florescence.

The other Czechs approached him and spoke in quick-fire tones as if to prevent The Supervisor and the other Slavs from hearing their language. Maury nodded and said that he understood. They replied that he had a strange accent and asked if he was from the countryside of Slovakia. Maury said no. He told them he was a Czech, but he was not born there. They asked him where he was born, and he said he honestly did not know. They did not believe him and asked again and more forcefully and without humor. He replied France because that was his mother's first language and his, too. Although, he could not remember being there. Thus, he was distrusted and accepted by his co-workers. He was given a mop in one hand and a broom in the other and fastened a belt across his belly with several cleaning accoutrements. His favorite was a squirt bottle with a blue foaming liquid that entranced him. Euphoria erupted through him as he imagined himself a villain in a comic book who had just invented the chemical that would unhinge his debonair superhero rival and give him access to all the money in the world. But then what? He frowned; it was when he had asked that question that all adventures died for him. All the fabled leaders of history, all the magnificent superheroes, the supraphysical embodiment of their times. But then what?

He wondered if the villains never seemed to die because in the heart of the superhero, he did not want them to die. If he killed his enemy, he would have no meaning. So, the good nursed the evil along in order to survive. It was a circular paradox that he suspected was at the core of human suffering.

Maury smiled and placed the squirt bottle back in its holster and found a display case that the Croatian in the group had just shined. He looked deeply into it and could almost see John Wayne. Then the Croatian returned and told Maury to get to work or the fat supervisor would come. He only came when they were at rest no matter how hard they had worked before. Maury nodded to the reflection and with mop in hand began to work. Casting the mop's tattered ropes over the floor in sweeping, graceful waves. Occasionally, his reflection would gaze back from between mop sweeps and he saw the face of a hero. One aisle over the Croat cursed and beyond that the Czechs spit. The noises combined in euphonious harmony beneath the humming florescent lights.

The mop swished and Maury smiled. Any task could be endured with a certainty that it would change. That was the essence of his adventure, and he knew then of how in America hard lives are endured by soft people. He stared into his brief reflections and smiled while wondering if any of his fathers or his mother could see him now on the other side of a reflection, wherever that was. He mopped until the sound of the system hypnotized him and he became lost in a timeless Zen trance.

He wagged and swaggered his way through one-sixth of the total aisles of Walmart and mopped over the occasional smattering of chewing tobacco merged with gum and spit that had sealed on the floor. The man who had spit the tobacco was a customer who did so because he was sure that the niggers continued to work at Walmart at night. He wanted to ensure that they did their job, so every day he spat, and when he returned the next day, he would look for his glob of chewing tobacco and gum and then go tell a manager about the shoddy floors. His actions had led to four firings and three deportations. None of whom were black.

Maury saw the blob and thrust his mop over it, and it remained. He hit it again and again and again until each granite part arose within the tendrils of his mop and then he flushed it all in the brown water with a little soap. As he cranked the mop clean the cursing Croat emerged behind him and said that it was morning, and their work was done. It was time to go back for the review.

When Maury and the Croat returned everyone else was already lined up with their hands behind their backs while facing forward. The Supervisor stood in front of them while rising and falling back on his heels and inhaling impatient breaths that expanded his rotund stomach even more. He was early so they were late. It was the same thing he did every time a new Slav managed to slip through the U.S. border and into a Walmart. The Supervisor shouted at Maury.

"Well, well soldier. The Russians tell me that you ain't one of em, but you look like a communist and you smell like one from here, drinking that vodka shit on the job, huh? Well, communist, were you? I'm talking to you."

"I am not a Russian, you know this." The Supervisor smiled, he had wanted some resistance and he was terrified that none would be offered and that his authority would be wasted in front of his rows of trembling Slavs.

"No, I don't know no goddamn thing 'cept that you late and I know it ain't because you working your pasty ass too much either. I seen you back there dogging it in all those aisles. What is your name, comrade?"

"I am not Russian." Maury implored The Supervisor to understand. He then sensed something vicious that he was too confused to comprehend so he detached himself from his body and observed what was happening to him. A skill he had previously honed to avoid pain like he was fated to endure in the next moment.

"I didn't ask for another one of your lies, I asked for your fucking name. You speake ze English, you fucking Nazi, or did they skip that lesson in re-education camp?"

"My name is Maury."

"Maury?"

Maury paused, uncertain about what to do next. He continued to watch himself from outside his body. Macabrely curious as to what would happen.

"Maury? Your fucking name is Maury? Hell boy, that almost sounds like a nigger name, and I think you just might be dumber than them. You think that, Maaaurry, do you, do you think that you're dumber than a nigger?"

Inside Maury's skull he screeched for a solution. He needed the money. From far above the part of Maury that was observing the situation whispered in his ear that a warm bed and a hot meal were worth enduring almost anything, that this man was nothing, a totalitarian sliver in the breadbasket of democracy, relax, to resist evil is to become evil, do not resist and he will go away. However, Maury could never listen to his pragmatic side. It was what propelled him through the world and brought him to this moment. With an internal snarl he growled back at his pragmatic self to be quiet and let human dignity rule the day.

"I do not know what a nigger is," he said. Then he clicked his heels and stood at attention like he imagined all American soldiers doing.

"Don't know what a nigger is. Well, how about that boys?" The Supervisor shouted towards the other Slavs, but they knew by this time to avoid eye contact and that a warm bed and a hot meal were the reward for indifference. "Don't know what a nigger is, huh? Well, should I be the fucking one to tell you, a nigger is a thing that your dumb communist ass is dumber than, does that explain it to you?" The Supervisor was very close to Maury now, he could taste his last meal without inhaling.

Maury's eyes twitched with glee and his mouth trembled with amusement. "Does that mean that you are a nigger, sir?"

"What?" His mustache inflated in an expansive puff, casting off flakes of dander like sexless, dying mayflies.

"Well, sir, I am dumber than a nigger, and we are all stupid Slavs in this room, except for you, sir, of course. So, I was wondering if you are a nigger, sir? Is that the definition." Maury felt The Supervisor's inhalation.

"No, I am not a nigger, you stupid fucking pinko, rusky bastard, and don't you dare say that again or I will send you on the first fucking ship back to Moscow."

"Ok, you are not a nigger. I just need help speaking me English, too many new words to learn."

The Supervisor paused; his authority had been taken from him with the flicker of a sentence. "Get in line with the other Russians."

"I am not a Russian." Maury was curious as to how far he could push the situation and he was certain that at least this far was absolutely safe. The Supervisor had lost his comfort and needed a way to regain his footing, some tool to hoist himself on.

"Ok then, what is it that you think you are? Tell the class. I'm sure the other Russians are eager to hear how you are better than them." A light flickered up The Supervisor's spine as he remembered his high school football days and that his coach had done this to him.

"Well, sir, since I no speakee the English much good, I think that I am a nigger."

The Supervisor thought of his grandfather and was enraged that Maury was sullying his concept of nigger. He panicked again, he needed space, time to think, to move, recover.

"Get the fuck back in line." He said softly and with menace so only Maury could hear.

Maury responded much more loudly. "Certainly sir, thank you for the compliment."

The Supervisor began droning about quality reports, action-item lists, the future of the store and then the future of the Walmart corporation. The whole time his eyes were fastened just above

Maury's chest. Maury reciprocated by staring directly into his eyes. The speech continued in what was now a pleasant Southern drawl that was interrupted only when The Supervisor's eyes met Maury's. Then he stuttered, incapable of subduing so much rage. Doubts would flint in his mind: What if his boss had seen him lose control of Maury like that? He would never promote him to manager of the daytime blacks. It was too dangerous. He had to remain calm so he looked again into Maury's chest.

The speech concluded and The Supervisor hurried out of the room. Before the plastic doors finished their third swing the men were outside and a plastic flask of vodka was unleashed. First sip to Maury and then the rest consumed by the Russians amongst themselves as the whole group walked to the bus stop to catch the first post-dawn express back to the transient motel where they would drink and sleep the shift and all its crushing exhaustion into oblivion.

They all boarded the bus and then it rattled through the Atlanta dawn. Maury sleepily looked out the window and saw two silhouettes. High on low-grade vodka, two men were fighting without weapons under a rusty red bridge. One figure dashed towards the other in a drunken fury and the other one climbed on top and thrust his fist seemingly through his head and into the ground. The punch broke his finger again. The bus passed by and then Maury slept in short, mechanical bursts. Beneath the bridge the narrative of the silhouettes continued. The men were vagrants and insane. They had long ago forgotten how to recognize the pungent redolence of piss clinging to their pants and traces of scat encrusted between their porcelain thighs mottled with black hair. Their fight was over a woman. She stood in the close shadows and swayed and clapped while giving a two-toothed grin to the combatants. The winner would have her that day. She would then lie beside him and go with her knight in shining armor to the circuit of food kitchens. She licked her lips and swayed while hollering a drunkard's laughter into the morning light.

She rubbed her hands over her sandpaper skin and cackled with delight at the sound of a fist into the skull of an already unconscious man. The silhouette on top hit him again and then had a different idea and bit his ankle and peeled off a chunk of skin that smoothly glided off the muscle like the peel of a mandarin orange. With the grace of a master chef's knife, he flicked his head to the sky and the skin was his. He chomped the flesh down while she wailed into the night.

Exhausted and hungry he went to the woman he earned who eagerly took him and they went to the ground. She removed his dick without taking off any clothes. With granite hands and dementia tremor strokes she aroused him to life while he shut his eyes and slept. Then, beneath the arch of the rusty red bridge a new silhouette was forged as the moribund forms merged together while riding and fucking.

When the yellow-tinted cum finally escaped his body and entered her rusty loins that had been plowed with the infertile salt of so much disease, Maury was asleep in bed and they were in shadow. Maury felt the warm sun of the new day protect him like a blanket as he tried to dream a long-forgotten memory. To dream a dream away from where he was, a dream that would allow him to forget until the sun finally ducked away from the day and it would again be time to have a drink and go to Walmart to begin his struggle anew.

Verse 4

The setting sun looked Maury directly in the eye and told him to wake. He stretched and showered and marveled at the way the humidity made him feel wet. There were a few hours of darkness before he had to go to work. Below him the Russians were already drinking dirty vodka. They offered some to Maury but he had a code that coffee must come before alcohol. So, he went to the diner to quaff cup after refillable cup over mottled eggs and toast.

Patricia was there and seated alone. Maury said hello and asked her when it was that she slept.

"When I need to," she quietly said.

Maury interpreted this to mean never. "Still waiting for your big bright shining knight from Texas to carry you away in his cowboy hat?"

"Still waiting, guess I'll always wait."

He understood and scraped his eggs against his toast, faster and louder.

"Hey, Maury, Maury?"

He stopped eating and looked to her.

"You been around the world right? Do you think that death is something that comes to us when we don't want it to, something that comes when we got families and friends and it takes us? Or is it something that we wait for and we die when we are ready to? That it's what we really want even though we'd never say it to our families cause they always relying on us."

Maury paused and scraped a greasy egg shrapnel off his plate. "I don't know. All I do know is that I have seen too many deaths, and the other thing that I know is that death should never be done alone. That is the saddest thing. A death with strangers is better than a death alone." He finished speaking and took another sip from his cup of coffee even though he knew that it was empty. Maury continued, "we all die alone though, more or less, we all die and there ain't no way anyone else can know what is going on." Patricia's shoulders sank. "I know that I do not want to die alone because I have watched other people do it in the street, in the cold, and in the night."

"Guess I'll just keep waiting."

Maury looked at the clock. If he left now, he would have plenty of time to get ready for work. He paid the check in exact change and got up to leave.

"I must go to work now."

"You ain't gonna leave no tip?"

"I am sorry."

She was flustered. "Tip, you have to tip, you have to give a girl a little something extra for servin' you so nice and with a smile."

"Ah, I understand, I do not have enough money for charity, maybe later, when death and fortune ride side by side and take me away I will give all the money to the pretty girls in Atlanta who have been waiting for me their whole lives."

"Be a pretty long wait. Where you goin'?"

"I am going to work for a big, important American corporation."

"Working at Walmart with all the others, huh?"

"Yes."

She nodded and jabbed her cigarette out, poking the nicotine cinders to oblivion with pugnacious jabs. "Well, I've known a lot of men in my life and the one thing that I've learned is that some of the best paying jobs are also the worst, not a more pathetic thing in this world than a man with too much money and even more problems. Well, maybe I'm worse off, but who knows."

"That is something that I have trouble believing, but I think that I understand."

"Yeah, guess that it's just like the death thing, all depends on who is lookin' at it from which side." They paused and shared a poetic moment together that died too soon. "Well, anyway, if you see my Mr. Right on your way back tell him that I been waiting for him too long on this here stool."

"I will, take care Patricia." She winked under the kerosene burst of her lighter as another cigarette blazed while she sucked it to life between her fulsome, blooming lips.

Maury left Merv's and saw that the Slavs were gathering in the soft yellow dew of the Georgia night. He did not greet them and instead started towards his room to look over pictures of his mother and feel a bag of dirt he carried from Europe to remind him of why he was still here. When Maury was almost to his room a door opened behind him and a figure cut out a silhouette that blocked all light from the inside. Maury froze. He could not detect any human features on the figure.

"Evening, you one of the new Slavs on the block?"

Maury paused and struggled for a deep breath to explain to the figure his mixed ancestry and why he had come to America. Then he stopped and swallowed his breath for the figure in the doorway must have already known his story.

"Must be a strange life for you to show up here, in Atlanta, at this exact moment in time."

Maury did not understand and there was something off about the figure. A medicinal charge in the air.

"Why is all this so strange?"

"Don't know myself, I'm an American, not like you're trying to be. I was born and raised on the same cartoons as everybody else. All this just came naturally to me. I just don't know why I am here now in Atlanta, doing what I'm doing."

"What are you doing?"

The figure just snorted and then chuckled and then there was a long silence that quickly gave way to a lone cricket's shrill violin.

"There is a woman in that diner over there. She talks like you, in a strange way. I think she is waiting for you. She said to me once that she is waiting for Mr. Right or a cowboy hat. Maybe it is both things."

The figure responded by ducking his head. "I must go to work now. Good luck doing the things that you do."

"Thank you for the advice, take care." Maury looked at the figure for a long, hard moment and then he closed his eyes, and he was gone. The figure made Maury need to sleep and he rushed to his bed and tumbled into a dream.

In the dream Maury became a camera for a photojournalist in Africa. Seeing and remembering horrors. Limbs on bright, brown dirt. Men languishing in outdoor cages. Madness in the air. Then the dream had other dreams of horrors that haunted him like nesting mosquitos fornicating in his ear.

He felt scratching wool from a ski mask go over his face and then he looked down and saw a pistol with a silencer in his hand. Outside of the shadow there was a blind boy from Sudan sitting on a bed with his shirt off. Standing near him was a pedophile excitedly grabbing his own crotch. The blind child gently swayed and smiled and said the man in the room smelled good, like the strong flowers from home his mother boiled in water. The boy licked his thick lips and they glistened, and the pedophile could almost see his reflection. Then the pedophile sat next to him and took off his shirt revealing his pot belly and pickle tits. Again, the pedophile reached for his crotch and the sweat started to pour into the figure's ski mask. He began to stroke the silencer on his pistol.

There was no one for miles, it was an act of kindness for the little boy who remembered the smell of flowers from his mother's milk when she nestled a flower deeply in the crevice of her breasts. It was large and red and beautiful, he touched it as he suckled from her, feeling the white warm fluid cascade down his throat and inside of him.

Blindly he giggled into the air in a way that made the pedophile feel comfortable. The boy was his now. The boy had not lied. He was an only child and alone. The pedophile violently squeezed his crotch.

The figure above in the black ski mask saw all of this. He had seen too much to believe in God but sometimes thought of becoming one. He expanded out of the shadow and placed the pistol near the pedophile's forehead and shot him in the face. The pedophile fell backwards on the bed while his skull fragments showered over the blind little boy like flower petals. The boy smiled because he liked the metallic smell of a discharged bullet shell.

The pedophile's soft body fell softly beside the boy and emanated a few moments of warmth into the room. The boy grabbed his chest and felt his mother's long gone warmth flow over him, and he smiled wider than his eyes and licked his lips until they cast a pellucid reflection onto the figure who was busy washing his hands.

After, the body had been placed in the bathroom to dissolve in plastic bags. The figure stood above the boy and lovingly spit into a napkin and wiped the remaining blood and brain matter off his face the same way that the boy's mother had done when he ate cassava too quickly. He then tucked the boy into bed and placed the napkin in his pocket. He went to the closet and reached to the back, withdrawing a broad, canvas colored cowboy hat for his date with Patricia.

Verse 5

Maury stepped into Walmart listening to the cumulative echo of too many florescent lights that floated aloft and beyond his vision. Through the glass of The Supervisor's office a radio preacher's muffled evocations of Hell, brimstone, and faggots all writhing together seeped out. Maury looked for his reflection in that glass and paused to absorb the new face looking back. He had grown heavier and clean shaven. He looked to his eyes and tried to find the fire. They were weaker now than in his optimistic remembrances. Suddenly, The Supervisor looked back through the reflection with a malicious smile that Maury could feel like an icy warmth.

Deep inside he was grabbed by a new fear for which he had no words in any language. He could not break free. This fear was worse than when a smaller man had reached above to make Maury kiss the mouth of a pistol before taking his money and making Maury give thanks for leaving him with his life.

The Slavs conglomerated in a still mass and exchanged esoteric greetings and jokes from homelands only acutely remembered now that they were all together. The Croat produced a bottle of Evian and smiled as he wafted the low-grade vodka under his nose. The arrival of The Supervisor was eminent, so The Croat took a long, trembling swig while gently squeezing the bottle at the end to chase away any remaining sobriety. With a palsy twitch he removed the bottle from his mouth and captured the remaining crystal drops on his seven-day growth of beard.

Other plastic Evian bottles passed from mouth to mouth while swapping spit and bacteria that writhed and died in the vodka's palpable ether. Only when this ritual was complete could they feel free to begin their working day in the false light of Walmart's dusk.

The Supervisor strode before them as they settled into formation and sniffed the air for the palpable remnants of last night's booze and today's euphoria.

"I've been here a long time and I've seen too many of you to remember, by now, boy you better believe me, by now, you alls look pretty much the same to me." He finished speaking and cleared his throat of phlegm. He swirled it around in his mouth, tasting it and hating it before spitting it on the floor in a way that looked like he had practiced this moment before, because he had. "Line up." He barked through the raspy remnants of the heap of biology in his mouth. "You." He pointed to Maury with his ring finger. The lone wedding band now showed the faded color from the false gold he had given to his wife. "You, you there."

Maury felt the eyes of his compatriots boring dozens of little holes into the back of his neck and compelling him to speak.

"Yes. Yes, I am here."

"Yes Sir!" He shouted. His voice had been infused with belligerence.

Maury sighed before continuing. "Yes . . . sir? What may I do with y'all."

"Y'all huh, son of the south huh, you northern fucks. Look there, look at the floor, think you can tell me what the fuck is there boy?"

Maury glared at The Supervisor's expectorate. "I do not know, what is there . . . sir." The eyes stopped penetrating Maury's neck and resumed their full attention to The Supervisor.

"That is some filthy Slavic shit right there. How do you think it got there, never had something like this before, so how you think that it got there?"

"I do not know . . . sir, I am not a management at Walmart."

"Oh, so you think a management did it, huh? When are you going to learn English? You are that stupid. Is that why your country is over there and mine is over here?"

"I do not understand, sir?"

The Supervisor paused and glanced at his watch. He was behind his own schedule.

"Well, it's all really simple. See if you can stay with me. That, you see that?" He pointed to the floor where the glob of expectorate was beginning to harden with flakes of black seeming to crystalize in the light. "That is a disgusting blob of shit that I ain't never seen before." He unfurled his fingers from their nascent arthritis and relished the pain and then did it again to put himself in the right state of mind. "And here I am looking at you, and I got to, I just got to put two and two together and think that one disgusting blob of shit that I ain't never seen before has come from another blob of shit that I never want to see again."

Maury paused, thinking to speak, his memory dipped its fingers into a stream of country hits of lost love and love never had and then reached deeper to feel the songs of betrayal and patriotism. When the hand emerged from the stream it came up empty.

"Sir, I don't understand, sir." Maury said. The whole room could have devoured Maury in that moment as the singular cause not only of the shimmering stack of spit on the floor but for all of life's dirty transgressions that had culminated in this point they were now enduring.

"Clean it up."

"What?"

"Clean it up, now, and the next time you forget English and don't call me sir, I won't do a fucking thing about it, but I will call my buddies at immigration and send a few of your friends here packing to wherever the fuck they came from. Now, I will speak slow so that your duuummmb, little ears can understand everything I have to say. C-L-E-A-N I-T U-P."

Maury quickly dashed to find a mop. Something he could not understand had happened.

"No! Where the hell are you going?"

"Sir, a mop, sir. I need to get a mop."

"What you need a mop for? It ain't that big. Clean it up with what you brought."

"Sir?"

"I speaking too funny for you or what? Your job is to come prepared for work. Your job is to not spit your fucking Slavic shit on my floor. Clean it up with what you brought. And do it now or immigration will come to check out the paper of some of you fellows."

"Sir, I did not bring anything, sir."

"I see. So, the new guy doesn't come to work prepared and don't care 'bout spitting on the floor. I tell you, son, I got a real bad feeling 'bout you, but I'm a good Christian lad, something you ain't ever gonna know, so I gonna be real nice cause you caught me in a good mood today. I'm gonna let you clean it up best way you can think of using the filthy clothes on your back."

The warehouse paused and waited. Then they waited some more. The Supervisor silently glanced at his watch and all on the floor were silent. In the rafters above a moth, disoriented and brought to the store in a shipment of discount children's dresses for church services and preschool graduations, fluttered skyward in a suicide dash to the ceiling, towards the light, towards the sun, wherever moths go when they leave the sight of man. It went higher and then smashed against the light. Stunned and surprised it fluttered back down to recoup its strength and go again. When the safety of rusting steel approached the moth with the scent of decaying iron and the coolness of a windswept elevation, it found that half of its legs were ensnarled in the invisible grasp of a female spider who was no longer fertile and waiting to die. She rushed out onto her dilapidated web and lunged into the soft furry stomach of the moth and injected it with her flesh-dissolving poison that grew in potency as her life neared its ninety-day expiration. The moth quivered in a vestigial instinct that would never go away from doomed life and lunged back towards the light above that quietly hummed its synthetic tune that had been refined to human perfection by chemistry and commerce. Then the moth perished, and the few neurons of the spider fired in simultaneous satisfaction as the insect began its inevitable process of being sucked dry.

Down below Maury had removed his shirt and exposed his massive physique that was too much strength to be carried by one man as he used his shirt to scrub up the remnants of The Supervisor's noxious human substance. Pushing his nail through the thinning fabric to scrape the dried edges that tenaciously clung to the gray cement. His back moved, drifted, and sweated. He was massive, powerful, and reduced to subjugation. The Supervisor grinned above. He imagined himself whipping Maury as his ancestors had done to others until the spot on the floor became completely clean and the stain of his resistance was removed from the memory of all who stood watching.

Maury finished his task and scurried back to his place in line and put his shirt back on while trying to avoid feeling the wet spot he just cleaned. It could not be avoided and so he quivered with revulsion and calculated just what the value of a hard day's work meant in this new land.

"Very good, see, look what a good job you can do, boy, just need the proper motivation. Now, if I catch you, or any of you other lazy bastards spitting on my floor you are all going back to whatever shithole you crawled out of and have to explain to your whore sisters and crying mothers 'bout why those few hundred dollars buying heat for the winter went away. You won't have anything to say 'bout that will you?" He waited for an answer and then continued. "Now, we're late, but a man ain't nothing without his routine, keeps him sane and sober. Onto the song. Who do you love?"

All were silent.

"I said, who do you love?"

Maury screeched out first and loudest, I LOVE WALMART YES I DO, and then his voice gave out before the remainder of the song rose from the viscera of the rest of the men. It was an archaic cry that in previous generations would have been saved for glorious slaughter in battle and the funerals of friends. They all sang the company song together in a spattering of languages and a dozen accents. A motley gospel choir singing their praises for the company; singing in boisterous competition to each other; louder and louder until the steel rafters above vibrated the song through the sensitive pads of the spider who paused to take note before again resuming her meal. In a time before she would have wrapped the moth and saved it for later but now her instinct prohibited it. She ate for the pleasure of it and savored the liquified organs and flesh of another who happened to stumble his way to her because he had failed to fly oh so high above her.

Verse 6

"Evening, Patricia. Mind if I take a seat?" The dapper stranger lowered himself onto the cracked, black vinyl.

Patricia looked at him and held her cigarette drag inside until the methane seared her chest and rolled like fire back up her throat. She coughed. As she released the smoke, she knew that he was the one she had been waiting for all this time.

"Feel free to sit, stranger. How you know my name when I don't yet have the privilege?"

"A little elf said that you would be sitting here."

She exhaled another plume and looked at it cast into the light and the face of Maury emerged and she knew exactly which elf had crossed his path.

"Maury," she said to herself.

"I'm sorry?" the Stranger replied.

"The elf, must have been a giant."

"Oh, he was."

"Well, funny the way everything works out. Do you believe in destiny?" She extended her sultry hand, limp and vulnerable so that he would have to take it, to rescue it and smell it, to kiss it and lick its scars, then, after all had subsided, he could fall in love.

"No ma'am, I do not."

"Not very romantic, are you?"

"I can be." Gingerly he stroked her fingers while probing their gaps and twisting the solid gold band around her thumb. Beneath the ring a lightning bolt scar emanated in all directions. It was deep and purple and had healed long ago and was acutely felt. He rubbed the scar against her bone, and she trembled in pain, almost cumming.

"Don't," she said, her voice weak. She drew his hand to her sloppily painted lips. Meekly she kissed his hand and closed her eyes as his scent overwhelmed her. An admixture, a hidden aroma below the meaning. The cologne was thick and expensive, one of the Italian ones. This much Patricia could know. Yet beneath it, beneath there was something else, the bitter, sticky sweetness of stale blood left to fallow like the acrid sugar she had whiffed off the tips of syphilitic cocks. Astonished and in love she turned his hand over and inspected him for decay, some gangrenous sprout or a scab shielding its puss from the world. There was nothing. The man simply reeked of death, and she was in love.

"Well, sir, must say that I've never met a man quite like yourself." She giggled like a once-loved and never-rejected schoolgirl. "You mind telling me what you call yourself?"

"Clarence," he replied. His voice unintentionally boomed in the room. "And that is all that you will ever need to know."

Grits grizzled and steaks fried. Demented giant flies jumped from margarine to butter and then through the vent. Patricia and Clarence snuggled together like newborn saviors. Love without the disgrace of puberty. They nestled closely as the other whores entered the building and looked over in envious awe at the couple. Around the cafe gentle whispers clicked and creaked. Gossip swirled around Patricia who hungrily cast her thumb over her loins. Her tongue yearned to stretch and plumb the depths of his heart. She was pulsing with a million living HIV viruses waiting to spread their seed and live again in the death of another. He was like her, too. She knew it.

"Thank you, thank you, Clarence. I'll be sure to thank our magical little elf as well, wouldn't be polite not to."

Back in Walmart: The labor force had been divided between the Eastern Europeans who moved to the front to shelve, mop, fidget, and adjust. The Russians remained in the back and hauled and moved and cursed.

Maury was told he had been demoted to the status of a Russian, just for the night, and if Maury failed to do his tasks correctly and to an inscrutable liking The Supervisor vowed that he would have one of the Russians deported before the next day had died. Maury's task was to sift through the garbage of the McDonald's that was inside the Walmart and caged off from the rest of the store to recover all waste materials visually depicting a plastic toy from the upcoming Disney film. Maury hadn't enjoyed a Disney film since 'Bambi' and wished that in that film they had killed the father instead.

The Supervisor placed him directly in front of the window to give the sense that he was always being watched and he was but for the times when The Supervisor ducked his head to read a short article from his glossy oversized sports magazine about next year's winners and this year's losers. If only the gamblers were the ones who controlled fate the world would make so much more sense.

The sound of trash squealing from plastic rubbing against plastic beat into Maury's ears and made him tremble. It was a sound connected to an activity, a sound of degradation, a sound that signaled his descent from the world of the Slavs to the world of the Russians. Where had his compatriots been for him?

When his work sentence was handed out by The Supervisor the Russians giggled and then the rest of them followed in some

Old-World natural order that Maury had struggled to flee. Maury held the nascent rot of a quarter pounder with cheese that was half-eaten and not enjoyed. *One of the Americans must have gone on a diet,* he thought and plunged his hand beneath to extract a piece of cardboard that Maury thought could be used again.

His hand plunged deeper amidst hardened fries that burrowed into his skin, soft cups covered in wax that burst out pockets of sticky liquid. Each type of trash found companionship with its own, like fossils in sedimentary rock. He looked to the Russians and thought of the others and wondered if all of us are here because we must be or because we want to be. His arm grazed another cup of soda, and he grimaced as the fluid surrounded his hand and washed the piece of cardboard he was trying to recover away. He wondered why McDonald's had not recovered all the material it could during business hours. Oh well, his hand went deeper, and his sleeves were drenched with ketchup and flecks of dissolving onions. He gazed through The Supervisor's window and The Supervisor was looking back. Maury thought that he would have been bored watching himself hours ago.

Bag after bag was opened and he winced in pain as the plastic handles uncoiled and hissed at him. He could quit, he thought. But then what? Never had he been able to purge his passions of the romance of rebellion. Master and servant, soldier and peasant, president and population. Now this fat bastard, middle manager, and Slav. Rebellion was a wonderful thing until the next day. Then what? The day after he would be hungry and a day after that he would be homeless. He did not come here to fail. Whyever he was here he would triumph. No, he could not afford to quit. The thought that he was working only to afford sleep in a shelter assaulted his sensibilities and then he forced it away while being distracted by a hardened bun that was saturated murder-red with ketchup.

That morning on the bus ride home, Maury clawed his flesh until it glowed in sanguine halos. The night had been long and, in the end, pointless. When his shift ended The Supervisor said that only cans could be returned for cash, cans only and that he must be dumber than the fucking Russians so he did not know where he would put him. It was a moment that stretched his soul skintight over a granite canvas, ready to snap. The manacles of civility that held other men so tenuously away from his violence nearly shattered. In his ideal mirror of memory, he had slaughtered The Supervisor, bludgeoning him and then discarding his immediately rotting Irish corpse with the mounds of French fries and piles of processed patties. In his mind's eye, he and his Slavic brothers looted Walmart until it was a barren pile of shelves with only the stale florescent lights remaining. Then they all returned to the shroud of black forests that sprung up in the parking lot overnight and reunited with unspoken abandon for a howling party preceding the sacred conclave ascension of a new king.

Maury snapped back to life and remembered what actually happened. His confederates stood stoically in line and the Russians released a communal snort. The others, the Eastern Europeans, stood soberly still.

Maury could not condemn them as he was now one of them. Life here meant more to all of them than any single act of degradation. Still, in his remembrance the real and imagined would fuse into one. He recalled the enthusiastic acts of a cruel man and the betrayal of a culture that was never rightfully his.

When the bus entered the final stop his arms were coruscated with droplets of blood-red ketchup. The stench of the McDonald's bags would not leave him. Even after he showered, he would sniff his arms and remember the stench. He would remember that smell for the rest of his life and he wryly noted this while plucking offending whiskers out of his mustache on his way to bed as he passed the tall, slender strength of Patricia's silhouette in the dusty dawn overshadowed by the lone ranger hat and body chiaroscuro of her new man and love. That man would kill three more convicted child molesters over the next few days. A personal record in which all significance would be lost the moment when Patricia told him that she had given him her disease and that there was nothing left to do in life, indeed had never been anything greater to do, than to die together.

They inhaled and heaved long, sickly, death-scented breaths from each other in their dank bed saturated with fleeing sweat. Death's blossom had started to bloom.

Verse 7

Sometime in the next week Maury awoke while counting the hours he had worked and calculating the wealth he would need to escape his past and be born again in a nation that was not his. He wondered why Africans were born in Africa, Europeans in Europe, Chinese in China and so on. He imagined clicking gods far away studying their own singularly confusing creation with varying degrees of magnification. At level ten they see the pumping flow of history through the veins of power and sublimation. Level one hundred they see the inevitable tide of culture rising over geography and surmounting towering mountains and damming unfordable rivers. Language and humanity collided, and the gift of culture gave texture to individual screaming lives born into the cosmic vacuum back at level one. Then one click more and the addition of another lens: level one-thousand. They see destiny confused as an individual aspiration. A person confused as to the implacable nature of life while concocting ways to survive and repaint death with the nuanced conditions of the self and the family. To the gods there were as many colors as people and all the people seemed to do was to create more of their own. Then one more click, this one a stubborn lens and they were taken to level one-hundred-thousand where genes vied for expression and cancer flourished when it was given the chance to breathe in a relaxed inhalation of tobacco. Flourishing in oblivion to the causes of their life, a sea of carp in a smaller dimension curiously turned when the hand of an individual emerged from the shimmering blue of the third dimension and granted a cancer growth or squashed bacteria from existence with a stream of suffering. Then owners of the hands looked away and conferred with each other, never speaking, feeling a bliss known previously in the recesses of the mad scientist skulls after the first nuclear test when their surefire theory had been put to practice and the unknown became irrevocably stained with new shades of darkness surrounding glass sired from sand. The gods had conferred, and they agreed that they had created a fine thing indeed.

Maury stared into the ceiling and was becoming blissfully certain that his dreams were melding with his waking life and that this is what he had struggled to do all along. He closed his eyes in an elongated blink and visualized the Walmart hours ahead.

The job imposed its identity on him and now routine had taken over. Wake before dusk and go to the never-ending day of warehouse life. Scrub, shelf, sweat, and remember to never curse. He used to count and run the hours through his head while calculating a living wage on his fingers. Then hours became florescent days, and each day had a particular price not in time spent but in money earned. Every day he was accumulating something, a stash of cash fastidiously hidden in the only bank he trusted that doubled as the mattress where he slept. He was on the border of no longer being young. His time was his most valuable commodity and he gave it freely. But now he worried that he had forgotten something. The choice he had made to leave the failed life in Europe to come here for something different, some goal that would dissipate into the whirling ash of industrial ether if he ever said it aloud. What he wanted was impossible and this made him want it even more.

Emboldened, he showered to prepare for work and sniffed his arm after a scrub of soap to rediscover the illusory stench of McDonald's trash he could not let himself forget. He opened the door to greet the dwindling day and saw Patricia's lone cowboy lighting up a patch of cement with incessant puffs of a cigarette. Maury wondered where cinema ended and life began and descended the stairs to speak to someone new, someone with whom he could be completely honest because the lone cowboy could not possibly care about the banal struggles of an illegal immigrant.

"Howdy, neighbor. Still here? Still standing tall like the cowboys in those movies?" Maury forced a smile and then a laugh. The previous evening the lone cowboy had executed another potential child-molester. This one was a family man who had the raw temerity to continue speaking of his children and lovely wife long after he had been shot in the neck.

"Still standing and still here. That's the way it has to be sometimes."

The air stood defiant and gelatinous while condensing in rolling slides atop their noses. They spoke in routine platitudes both had heard said before by respectable members of Southern society. Maury ducked under the stairs to remain in the shadow so that he could see through the penumbra cast across his face by the cowboy hat that stood too tall. Both were large men. Maury was bigger. Maury would always be bigger and that was his way.

He tipped his hat to Maury and lurched up on the toes of his cowboy boots. "What you been up to these days? A little buck like you ought to have a reason to hang round here, shouldn't he?" He was half-jealous because of Patricia and fully worried that any transient at the hotel who lingered too long would notice his weekly sessions of violence and call the police.

"I got a job. I live in the American dream."

"A job, eh?" He hit him on the shoulder, "Hell, knew things would pick up sooner or later. They pick up for you they gonna pick up for everyone. Where you been working at?"

"Walmart. It is a big store, giant store, do you know it?"

"Walmart? That ain't the American dream. That there is the American nightmare."

Maury released tenuous glances towards the Russians and the Slavs standing at the bus stop. He had grown accustomed to their gruff companionship and silent presence that he now knew as camaraderie. The cowboy prodding into his life made him feel uncomfortable. He was discovering inadequacy when before he had known only progress.

"They treat you pretty good over there?"

"My boss is OK, he a good guy." The hair on Maury's neck revolted and stood at attention, making him take note that he was in great peril. "Well, thank you, good talking, I have to go for my bus." Maury turned away from the cowboy silhouette underneath his room and started to walk to the bus stop. Abruptly, he was halted by a firm grasp from the cowboy's hand.

"Yes," Maury said, eyes blinking wide.

"I just couldn't let you go 'fore I told you thanks for introducing me to Patricia." His drawl stretched his words so long that they nearly snapped from comprehension in Maury's skull.

"Patricia, yes." It returned to him. All of it. His life before. The soul who knew only resistance and becoming. "Very dark girl, I like her a lot."

"Yeah, she come off that way in the get go, but after you get to know her a little, she turns out to be just fine. In fact," he checked the periphery of his vision for eavesdroppers, "tonight, I'm gonna ask her to be my lady, we gonna be man and wife."

Maury stood stunned. How much time had elapsed since Joe, the coffee shop, the whores, this out of place cowboy? It couldn't have been that long, only the job had changed and in Maury's acceptance of it an eternity ensued but now he realized and clasped his hands in excited triumph. "She was waiting for her man; she waits no more because she has you."

"Well, yeah, you could say that."

"Marvelous, fantastic things these are. Good work, mazel tov, as the Jews in New York are saying."

"Well gee, never known a Jew, guess I never hated one either."

The sound of puffing exhaust awakened Maury to the presence of the bus. He turned, waving and yelling behind him, and raced towards it with long strides that felt like he was running through stone as he recalled his life. The love he cherished within it and the monolithic terror he would now have to endure. Yes, something had changed since he had come to America and now it would change again.

He grunted at his colleagues as he entered the bus, and they grunted back. It was a new day, rife with optimism and change. Maury looked behind the bus and saw himself ascending in the form of a puff of exhaust spreading towards the sun. Something was deeply remembered, and he went to Walmart to work with a smile on his face and a vision of blue infinity just past the asphalt horizon. He even saw ahead of the bobbing head of the bus driver that seemed to whistle a happy tune from time to time.

The cowboy stood in silhouette in the shadows. His hat no longer cutting an image from the light. He was waiting for Patricia with a ring in a velvet box dampened by his sweaty hand. His life had been one of exhilaration over the deaths of others. Before, when he had more honor in his killing, he told people he was a veteran. Ahh, it was a good life that he had lived though. Fraught with peril, love, and at last disease. The killing meant little now. It did not move his heart to excitement as it should have and as it used to, like he imagined that it always would.

ricia though, she was new and something spectacular. The
_nate longing one feels only with the onset of lust during ado-
lescence when girls menstruate and boys understand the reason
that Adam eventually wore a fig leaf in the presence of Eve. It was
a good feeling and true to the flesh and invigorating to the spirit.
He tipped his hat and stroked the velvet on the box back and forth
while thinking of tides and seasons and change. Patricia would
make him happy.

In the diner she swiveled around in her chair and looked out the
window at his silhouette beneath the iron stairs. It was out of place
like a homeless person in suburbia. Gingerly, she lurched forward
and caught herself and exited through the door to approach her
destiny and his. Then it would be their destiny and their death too
that they could have and hold forever as man and wife.

As she approached, her lithe body struggled against her flapping
white shirt that was torn at the shoulder. She saw him and loved him.
It was the moment to end their suffering and begin their miraculous
death together. She placed herself in some other time fused with
nobility, a chivalrous Europe, not too far away. A western outpost
after the Indians had been cleared and the ground trembled with
fertility. Yes, that suited her, nothing spectacular or that had not
been done but a good life and something important. A forerunner in
manifest destiny. She walked, sulked, and stumbled, catching herself
with a cough before she gave a laugh that she could only know on
the inside.

He said, "Evening, stranger. You sure look serious tonight."
She answered, "These are serious times."
"Haven't they always been?"

"True."

"Still, I have to say that you are the prettiest gal this side of heaven."

"That where we are?"

He paused and licked his lips a few times until they turned cherry red in the gulch of the parking lot. "You sure are inquisitive tonight, aren't you?"

He looked down and she caught his arm by the wrist. He clenched his fist until it trembled white with his ring, their ring, concealed inside.

"You're so tense. How bout we do something relaxing tonight, just you and me, what do you say?" She stroked his hand and his muscle relaxed and his fingers parted revealing a glimmer to the ring case inside. She saw it and knew it and her pupils expanded in a junky's delight.

"That sounds fine, just fine."

They walked the short distance into his room and, under her breath so that only she could hear, she whispered, "Mamma, you'd be so proud."

"What was that darling?"

"Nothing, sug. I was just thinking that you look so fine." They entered his room and she shut the door behind them. Inside a wet tarp of perspiration and blood clung to the air. In the corner the Sudanese boy betrayed his autism and recognized the new stranger and what she had to give to his adopted father, and he shrieked out into the dark room. "What was that?"

"That's just my boy."

She looked over in the dark, barely making out his shadow and moved closer, her feet suddenly burned as she stood where a pasty pedophile barely into middle age had fallen to his knees and sprayed the child with blood the night before. "Where did you find him, Vine City?"

"He's not like that, he's African."

"Ahh, I don't believe I've ever touched an African before." She stroked beads of stagnant sweat from his face. "Hello, what is your name?"

"Uhh, Patricia," he said, slapping an imaginary mosquito off his neck. "He don't speak too much, he's got a medical condition."

"What's that?"

"Autism."

"Don't think I know that; is it contagious?"

"No, no it ain't." He paused while searching for words. "You know Faulkner?"

"Now that's a name that sounds very familiar."

"Yeah, well, he's a pretty good author, one of the best, I've heard folks say, and he's got this great book that all the old timers like me have read."

"Ah, sug, you ain't that old."

"Right." He felt his age and her beauty lying dormant and shielded from the world by years of cigarettes and whiskey breath. "Well, he wrote this one book called *The Sound and the Fury*, and it's all about life before now and The South and such things. Anyway, there's this character named Benjy, and his world just don't make no sense, it's kind of a hard book because of Benjy, anyway, Benjy's world got no real sense of time, no past no future, he kind of insane but he isn't cause he feels things so intensely. Anyway, Benjy don't make no sense, like I was saying, until you see him in the book and think about him, and you think that he has this kind of disease. Anyway, that's what I think and I'm sure someone with a degree agrees. I think that Benjy has autism and I know my boy does."

"Oh, so his disease has a name. Does *he* have one?"

He looked down at the boy and wiped his sweat back over the dry spot Patricia had left. "Ask me that question a little later. We've got some important things to discuss."

"Ohhh, I think I like the sound of that. Well, it sure was a pleasure meeting you Mr. Autism, I hope to be seeing you shortly." She bowed in a long curtsy of Southern insincerity and was quickly swept away by the arm to the other room. Patricia and the cowboy spoke in quiet rapture as he told her of his pain and giving it to her so they could hold it aloft together while never touching the ground. They would speak over a mountain of things that night while Patricia smiled and supported. She never really heard his words. In his voice was the humbling parlance of a weakened man giving away all his trust, and she took it and swallowed it and never released his arm that held her sacred ring.

Back in Walmart: Maury trudged into work with the others who all maintained a perfect three day's growth of beard that never grew nor waned. He whistled the corporate mantra that they shouted every night in oscillating tones from his puckered lips. After the first salvo, Maury added a ragtime beat to it and increased pitch with volume. He felt the ire of his compatriots fly to the back of his neck and he did not care. He had embraced the American abyss. They were not his countrymen nor he theirs. They belonged nowhere and that was exactly what they had in common with the American people. It was not language or geography that made a Yankee Doodle Dandy. No, that was old Europe, clinging to its food and esoteric tongues and calling it language. What made an American was the knowledge that it is only possible to shine on oh-so-brightly without roots. Maury was going to be a star. He could be a faint one, but he would be a star. His companions could not forget the land that was innately theirs that they could never leave behind.

Maury had no such connection; he didn't need it. Life is in the present. History is written by the current generation for it is not in the chronicling of events that history interests us but in casting a bolt of meaning back through the eons immemorial so that now this moment, this time, is the greatest moment to have ever been. Inside Maury's skull his feet were swept off the cement floor in a gust of zero gravity and he flew up with the others around him who expanded from the pressure change until they popped in a discordant union. The variegated palette of their viscera coiling through the space. Maury quickly fled while the remains of the others were tangled in coils of brown and yellow and red. Occasionally, a purple organ emerged through the mass and caught Maury's attention before he was lifted off away and breathless towards a faint beacon of light far beyond the horizon.

Within Walmart and outside of Maury his whistle crescendoed from ear to ear in a joyful renunciation of his past and his peers. Maury smiled and thought that death is the annihilating scourge not merely of men. No, it is the scourge of civilizations and universes without names. It is the always-drowning abyss. Today, Maury felt good to have no future and no past. He felt good to be born again always floating in the ether of his mind.

Maury's whistling had roused The Supervisor from his well-worn office chair that had been reupholstered twice in sticky vinyl. He stroked the gray hairs in his mustache and tapped the desk with rhythmic thumps of his sausage fingers. Tonight would be fantastic; he had been waiting for it with the ardent sadism of vengeance long since denied.

He remembered sitting next to Mary Frances Early on her first day of his school's forced desegregation and having to face his father's great shame when he arrived home. His father was not a violent man but that night he gave him a beating he could still feel. The Supervisor massaged his shoulder from where the first blow had been.

His friends had pushed her though. Pulled her hair, pushed her forward and made the cement scrape her knees. They did all these things until they were older and donned those white sheets like something a kid would wear as a ghost on Halloween. Then they went and beat someone's husband to death before stringing him up from a tree.

The Supervisor felt his father had been right about him. He was too much of a pussy for the Klan. All his friends went on, graduated and became sheriffs and state senators while he had done nothing except earn his current station in life. Well, it was time for a change, time to become a remarkable man.

The Northerners had won, and the South had become an antebellum memory carried on only in the delusions of old women and little girls who thought like they were old. The North may have won but The South had not changed. Inertia was victory. The struggle was never really about white or black. The South had been born from agrarian dreams and so it was connected to the dust of the earth just as the banks of the north created skyscrapers to glorify their being. With agriculture it was always about power and submission. Who stood tall and close to God and who had their head smelling the Earth?

The Supervisor felt the surge of battle pulse in his throat and marched onto the floor to review his troops and wait for the Slavs to realize that he had decreased their numbers by a few the night before.

"Line up."

Maury was startled away from his whistling and hustled into formation. They all stood together in near silence but for the hum of florescence above. Maury was the last to notice and the first to speak.

"Where are they?" He whispered to himself. The first row of the formation had been occupied by three Ukrainian brothers, from a small town near Chernobyl, who had moved together because too many of their friends had perished from exotic forms of leukemia that existed only there, like an endangered species.

"Good question." The Supervisor responded, surprising Maury as if he had been present in his skull.

The previous morning at the conclusion of work The Supervisor had stared through the glass and saw his power eroded. The Slavs, these scurrilous bastards, were concerned only with their job and not with him. They had been performing their tasks with a dutiful efficiency that he did not believe existed within them. He had felt his personal dominion over them transform into corporate efficiency and this roused him to rage. He made a phone call to his high school buddy at immigration and told them that there were undocumented neighbors of his that he thought could be terrorists because of their brown eyes and hard language. Later, a black van had pulled before their house during the heat of a restless night. The three Ukrainian brothers were sleeping in two beds when the jarring strength of a knock that only those in power can produce jarred them all to their senses and compelled them to the door with each crashing cymbal of fist against wood. The oldest of the brothers opened the door ever so slightly and braced it with his shoulder because they were too poor to afford a safe neighborhood. In the future they dreamed that would change and they often wondered why the most violent neighborhoods in America did not have much worth stealing compared to all the rest.

"Yes." He said gingerly to the white man dressed in black standing under the wan illumination of a misty moon. Minutes later it was over and all of them were meekly tossed into the back of a giant van only indiscreet at night. Across the street, The Supervisor sat alone in his car sucking air through the pulsing cinders of the two-dollar cigars he brought out for special occasions like these. He smiled and licked his lips to find the flavor. This one was cherry.

He relayed the story at Walmart to the profound chagrin of his employees. Unwrapping the details like a flowing robe while he thumbed through a stack of index cards with the given addresses of everyone on the night crew. He told them that things were going to be different around here from now on and that their lives were a mere phone call from returning to the dank Eastern European hole from whence they came. After he finished his speech, he dismissed the crew and whimsically stroked his mustache and mulled over the reasons he had selected the three brothers. Perhaps it was their vulnerability, the quiet way in which they stuck together and did their job. Perhaps it is because they seemed to have the most to lose and so were a little desperate to please. Just can't respect a desperate man, doesn't matter what the situation is. Or maybe it was just because they stood in the front of the formation and were the first in his vision.

"Now, you boys remember, when you see those lights flashing through your window, it's the light of my nation's redemption, coming to carry you home, and you think when you're working, now, you think real good 'bout what you're doin', cause this is the face of the man who sent you packin', long way away, packin' back to where you boys rightfully belong."

th hushed steps he turned on his heels and went back to
ice. He started to flip through the glossy pages of low-grade
pornography while in his wake a miasma of terror dilated the
pupils and raised goosebumps across the collective flesh of the men
outside.

Maury went to the front of the store with his nerves shattered and his
sensibilities drowning in indignation. He had seen a man murdered
on the street before for nothing palatable, no gain, perhaps a dispute
of honor, and somehow that incident made more sense to him than
what had just happened. The brothers could have been killed and
the mood would not have changed. They had been sacrificed for a
purpose beyond explication. Now the brothers were myths to the
other employees and irrelevant to the future. Maury frowned and
began to sweat. He felt poison streaming from his heart. What had
happened should not have. He needed it explained.

"Why does he treat us in this way?"

Maury looked up from his mop; his complexion was further etiolated under the dim glare of florescence.

"You do not know?"

"I do not."

"How long have you been in this country?"

Maury thought and tried to come up with a number that matched
his memories. "I cannot remember, can't recall the time . . ." His
mind trailed away into some saccharine country western verse

"Do you know what a nigger is?"

"It is a black, no? It means a black."

"That is what I thought, and that is what the dictionary says. But
the word is very much more. Niggers are no longer the blacks, it is

a thing that never dies, it is in all nations, but here it is strongest, we are the new niggers."

"But I am not black."

"That is not what it means. Look at us. We are the worst things in this country. We run away and hope they never catch us because then we will have to go back, but we cannot go back because the Europeans want us less than the Americans do. Over there we are stupid Slavs, only criminals and pimps and murderers. Here, we are the lowest things because the Americans like their criminals. They have style and that means something here. We are the niggers because everyone in this country is superior to us, we were born into this nigger class, this nigger thing, it does not matter that we were born on another continent. We are not good enough for our own countries and we are barely tolerated here. That is what it is to be a nigger."

Maury paused to make sure that he understood everything. "So, a nigger is not a person. A nigger is a thing?"

"Yes, and we suffer because we were born to be niggers, even though we were born an ocean away."

The florescent hum punctuated the conversation and even steamed over the sound of the swooshing mops beneath their feet. Maury stared into his reflection on the floor. He had never been so low before. He had climbed the highest mountain he could find, and he used to believe that doing so was worth all the effort. If he fell from the tallest peak, he would die with the most glory and that is what he had always believed until another Slav, not a countryman but a brother to him here, had told him that there was no worse form of life than what he was born to be. An ineffable class of man that would never perish and never really live in the eyes of one more powerful.

Maury pondered, "What do you think their names was?"

Swoosh, the mop hurried back.

"Who?"

"The Ukrainian brothers."

"You should not believe in fairy tales; you were the child who sat closest to the old women when you were growing up, weren't you?"

Maury's cheeks pinched in mortification.

"Why believe The Supervisor? Does he have government powers? I do not know, but I do not think he would have his own people arrested. I do not think he can make the phone call to the high man in power. It would come here; it would come to him."

"You think?" he implored to Maury, optimistic that the Ukrainians had escaped and were out there pacing through the night.

"I think the only difference between America and the rest of the world is that the people believe in the justice of their own systems.

They are worse than the communists were in that regard. Always we had doubts, but the Americans are religious, they believe in their governments and themselves. They believe in them fully and that is why this country works."

"You think the Ukrainians are safe?" He looked at Maury between the flowing creases of sheets beneath his eyes. There were things he felt and things that he was certain he would never say.

"I do not know."

"Do you think that we are safe?"

"Only until the lights and the flashing and the men in black masks come before your door." Both smiled painfully and inwardly and continued to finish the night's work in a silence that stretched longer than the miles of neatly shelved items at bargain prices.

Verse 8

The cowboy and Patricia held each other on a bed half-clothed and embarrassed. A sporadic Doppler boom of a passing truck and the stomping of steel of a late-night reveler outside marked the passage of time for them. With the awkwardness of adolescents, they undressed without seeming to know what was at the end. Neither of them spoke about what was happening. Their sentiments had been lost and tucked in a bituminous bedrock of the psyche that required steady heat and pressure to expose their glow to each other.

Patricia needed him. She would be the aggressor. She was the one slowly dying with a lonely heart that ached for death. She struggled with his belt, and he feigned resistance, and she applied more effort to topple his will and make him consent through acquiescence. His belt buckle, an imitation of a victory rodeo belt, sparkled gaudily by day, but in the midst of a closed room and two sweating bodies, it lost its fire as if the oxygen was fleeing the room with every breath. She crawled closer to him and huffed exhalations into his panting mouth. He took her air and felt it against his skin like a new, perfectly fitting shirt. More Doppler booms from trucks passing by while she fought with his belt buckle until finally it relented, and she could join her man. She moved, sliding, and gliding atop him and smothered herself over his quickly rousing spirit. She let him grow inside of her as she felt her life unfurl. She moved to penetrate his barriers and grind his body to an orgasmic halt while whispers of remorse barely kissed his lips before they died in the air.

She felt her release within, and she hoped beyond maternal hope that she had impregnated him with her disease. He would give birth to their shared death. It was all he wanted, and she could smell it. Through all her memories she had known that the only thing worse than life itself was dying alone. Now she almost had a companion, a soulmate to walk down the last howling aisle from an existence of the flesh into the realm of other men's dreams.

She crawled to his side and with her nail scraped a long curve of crimson across his chest. She briefly worried that she had not infected him. She did not yet feel her death within him. She was scared that the disease was all still within her. Like a dog neglected beyond dehydration she lapped up the blood that barely trickled. She prayed to herself in gratitude. They would have many nights below a ceiling that hid the moon and the stars to feel comfortable. They had a love now that could only lead to their deaths. She was in heaven.

Outside of the room the buses of Atlanta roared and puffed and hurled people throughout the city. Maury was returning from Walmart with his head resting against the steamy glass of the bus window. He bobbed in and out of sleep and awakened into a dream. and believed it was consciousness. Sometimes he awoke in a panic feeling that he was in some other country and that the signs were riddled with scripts he could not read and that he was born again as a child in another place that was not the land of his birth.

When the bus stopped in front of the transient motel, he was more exhausted from his brief nap than he had been after work. He thought that the work was not that difficult. He had done much worse. Strained and lifted and bled. Sniffed rust and tasted oil.

He walked off the bus conscious and barely dreaming. The Russians and Croats from Walmart headed their separate ways to drink the same vodka. After work was a time for rejoicing and he knew that. Still, nothing seemed to be correct. Something was not happening that should have been. His feet scraped the earth as if they were made of iron and were magnetically being drawn to the core of everything. He was too tired to be living. He paused outside of the door of the lone cowboy. He almost said hello, until he closed his eyes in a prolonged blink, and when he awoke, he had had a dream that inside the cowboy and Patricia had found love and that soon it would be OK because they would be dead and their love would persist.

When Maury entered his room, he found a homeless man sleeping on his bed, covered in his own rags for a blanket. He checked the room number twice and then shut the door and hurled the bum across the room as if he were a skipping stone, before taking the bed that was rightfully his. He worked hard all night so he could sleep all day in this bed. No man was going to steal the fruit of his labor.

Maury was hard asleep when the homeless man awoke at noon and showered and shaved. He briefly thought of slicing Maury's throat and then searched his clothes for money. He couldn't take anything though. It was something about Maury. Confused, he left and gingerly shut the door on his way out back into the real world.

Maury slept and dreamt fantasies about real people. Life made sense when he was asleep. The underlying logic of humanity was known innately in his skull. He moved and connected with an intimacy he lacked in the waking world. Every night he fell in love. Every night he was the hero of a small stage and that much greater for it. He dreamt with divine wisdom.

Life was what worried him these days. Ever since Maury's mother first told him that dreams were the obvious answer to our past, he had been troubled by the waking world, as if each day had a key that only needed to be found.

He dreamed a dream of all his days. Of years distilled into their signature moment. That one occasion when all our blood and toil is proved to have been acts of wisdom or the cutest delusion. He swept over his personal history, the first fight he won and the last one he lost, losing his virginity to a girl who said that his cock felt like fire and wept before putting ice atop her pussy. Becoming an apprentice and giving himself to the dreams of an older man . . . then the betrayal and it was back to life with his mother who paid for all their meals with the company of a different man. Something about the French side of her that was irresistible. In his dream he grasped for a theme, something to connect his language and place with what he knew to be true. None of it aligned. He was a perpetual tourist. Not even a voyeur when the mirror looked back.

He awoke at dusk as Patricia choked on the air in silent ecstasy as she felt her disease leave her body and spread again to the corpus of her beloved. The disease flowed back and forth between them now. There was nothing to do but to wait and fuck, fuck and wait. Maury awoke to greet the night, exhausted. He showered in hot and cold bursts hoping that something would rouse his spirit. Nothing did.

He left the shower and heard a sharp wrap at the door and panicked thinking that the men in black had come to ship him on his way out of here and to wherever. His heart paused and then he opened the door. It was Patricia who was glowing in the crepuscular air with rivulets of cum trickling down her thigh.

Verse 8

She had come to thank Maury for giving her the greatest gift in the world. Love and death in a singular act. She called him a poet, a saint, a savior. He rubbed his eyes and tried to clear them of the sleep that would not leave. Deeply, he wanted to smile and to show his teeth and be grateful. He tried to understand what had happened and what she wanted and why she was here. If he were ever to ask her directly she would lie and summon the skills of her trade that taught her to know what men needed to hear and the lies they demanded of all women.

"What, what have I done to y'all?"

"I know . . ." she paused to light a cigarette and artfully send the smoke above Maury's skull. "I know that you did not intend to give me any of the gifts I have received. But I just want to tell you that I found my baby, he doesn't want to live anymore, he just wants to love me. He's perfect, y'know, Maury."

"Um, I am not from here. I do not know."

She soberly placed her hand on his chest.

Behind them the snooze alarm rang its second series of grating noises that was a polemic against anything beautiful. A death to harmony. Maury squeezed his brow once more. He had come to see his alarm clock as some lunatic bird that cried each dusk to rouse him to enter the never-ending-day of Walmart florescence. The noise continued to hammer at his skull. The same noise that daily tore millions from comfortable beds with their beautiful loves and ripped them asunder from nightmares and insipid dreams. The sound kept the country moving and intoned people to the obedient ritual of industry like a howling Buddhist chant.

Christ I'm lonely, Maury thought. "You will have to excuse me; I am going to be late for work. I am jumping in my boots with excitement that you have found what you wanted. Your American dream is because of me? No? Yes?"

"Yes, it is, sug." She blew three concise smoke rings into his apartment and finished them off with a circular kiss that made her cringe with lust. "If I were a different woman, I would certainly repay your kindness with the greatest Southern hospitality you could ever know."

"Why thank you, ma'am." His awkward English returned, and he again tripped over vowels and consonants while slipping through them all. Maury reached for a cigarette of his own and then Patricia gingerly shut the door. He didn't understand how Patricia could smoke outside. It seemed to Maury that smoking was the last American sin, so he lit and puffed indoors and marveled as the smoke spread over his clothes. He went to the curtain and timidly moved it aside to see what was there. Everything was as it should have been with trucks in a row and the Slavs being drawn from their temporary dwellings and into the night and to Walmart. Maury thought of Patricia. What did she mean, *repay my kindness*? Why is everything a debt here? Kindness is a duty. Spreading her legs is her duty. It is impossible to repay someone for doing their duty. He wondered what more was boiling under the glimmering white of her flesh. A marble perfection cracked only by the occasional mole that emerged from the dark and deep.

"Shit." Maury looked back to his clock, "I am going to be late." He extinguished his cigarette on the nearest piece of furniture, and excitedly finished getting dressed, as he stumbled out the door while whistling a corporate song to keep him company, as he raced to catch the dirty white bus coming under the day's dying sun.

About Andrew McGregor

*A*ndrew McGregor has an eclectic background in the not-for-profit and social enterprise worlds drawing from his expertise as a filmmaker, Grammy nominated bagpiper, inventor, writer, chess boxing champion, entrepreneur, frequent TEDx speaker, mentor, Highlands games athlete, photojournalist, magician, Curator of MindshareLA, and a founder of The Tiziano Project. He was named one of 'LA's 40 Most Interesting People' by *LA Weekly*, was part of a team that won the SXSW Interactive Award for Activism, won the 'Foreigner' division of an Independence Day Chess Tournament in Kazakhstan, he was featured in the Sports Section of the *NY Times*, and he has even received a Certificate of Appreciation from LA's City Council!

Fresh Ink Group

Independent Multi-media Publisher

Fresh Ink Group / Push Pull Press

Voice of Indie / GeezWriter

Hardcovers

Softcovers

All Ebook Formats

Audiobooks

Podcasts

Worldwide Distribution

Indie Author Services

Book Development, Editing, Proofing

Graphic/Cover Design

Video/Trailer Production

Website Creation

Social Media Marketing

Writing Contests

Writers' Blogs

Authors

Editors

Artists

Experts

Professionals

FreshInkGroup.com

info@FreshInkGroup.com

Twitter: @FreshInkGroup

Facebook.com/FreshInkGroup

LinkedIn: Fresh Ink Group

Fresh Ink Group
Guntersville

CPSIA information can be obtained
at www.ICGtesting.com
Printed in the USA
LVHW022136080423
743855LV00014B/1166